"Delphi..."

He spoke softly, but there was a hard gleam in his brown eyes, a tension in the way he was holding his lean muscular body that made her breathing go shallow and her skin grow warm. "I came as soon as I heard."

The familiarity of his voice, or rather the dizzying rush of adrenaline it produced, prodded at her already jangling nerves so that for a few moments she didn't take in his actual words, just the smoothness of the syllables. Then she stiffened.

What did he mean, as soon as he heard? Heard how? From whom?

What had she been thinking?

She should never have come here.

"How kind," she said coolly. "But you really didn't have to go to so much trouble."

"It was no trouble. I was in San Francisco closing a deal, so it was merely a slight diversion."

Pain scraped across her skin. *No change there, then*, she thought, a pulse of misery and anger beating in her throat. During the entire time she had known him, Omar was always closing a deal somewhere. It just so happened that today the deal was happening in San Francisco.

"A bit like our marriage," she said, tilting her chin.

Louise Fuller was a tomboy who hated pink and always wanted to be the prince—not the princess! Now she enjoys creating heroines who aren't pretty pushovers but are strong, believable women. Before writing for Harlequin, she studied literature and philosophy at university, then worked as a reporter on her local newspaper. She lives in Royal Tunbridge Wells with her impossibly handsome husband, Patrick, and their six children.

Books by Louise Fuller

Harlequin Presents

The Rules of His Baby Bargain
The Man She Should Have Married
Italian's Scandalous Marriage Plan
Beauty in the Billionaire's Bed
The Italian's Runaway Cinderella
Maid for the Greek's Ring

Christmas with a Billionaire

The Christmas She Married the Playboy

Visit the Author Profile page
at Harlequin.com for more titles.

Louise Fuller

THEIR DUBAI MARRIAGE MAKEOVER

Recycling programs for this product may not exist in your area.

ISBN-13: 978-1-335-58393-2

Their Dubai Marriage Makeover

For questions and comments about the quality of this book, please contact us at CustomerService@Harlequin.com.

Harlequin Enterprises ULC
22 Adelaide St. West, 41st Floor
Toronto, Ontario M5H 4E3, Canada
www.Harlequin.com

Printed in U.S.A.

THEIR DUBAI MARRIAGE MAKEOVER

To my mother-in-law, Ann Fuller.
May 11, 1935–February 25, 2022.
With love.

CHAPTER ONE

FLOPPING BACK AGAINST the scratchy hospital pillow, Delphi gritted her teeth. How much longer was she going to have to sit here?

She had no idea how long she had been waiting. Hospitals were like casinos. The longer you stayed, the harder it was to keep track of time. Annoyingly, her phone had run out of juice soon after she'd arrived, but Carole, the nurse who'd iced her bruised wrist, had looked at her as if she had grown horns when she'd asked if she could charge it.

Breathe, she told herself firmly.

Forcing her shoulders to relax, she inhaled in through her nose slowly, held her breath, counting to seven, and then exhaled through her mouth. She was supposed to make a whooshing sound, like a child blowing out the candles on a birthday cake, but she didn't want to think about her birthday right now. If she did, then she would think about Dan and her brothers and the ranch—

A wave of homesickness rolled through her, and she sat up straight, ignoring the jolt to her wrist. Carole had left the orange floral curtains slightly open and she stared through the gap.

It was the Fourth of July. She would have thought today of all days the hospital would be like a ghost town. That everyone would be meeting up with family and friends to eat charred burgers and their great-grandma's special potato salad.

But there were so many people milling around it might as well be that casino she'd thought about.

When she'd mentioned this to Dr Kelly, the doctor who had examined her, he'd rolled his eyes.

'It might be all burgers and potato salad for you, young lady, but this is the ER's busiest twenty-four hours of the year. You name it. We get it. Food poisoning. Dehydration. Sunstroke. Firework-related injuries,' he'd listed grumpily as he'd peered into her eyes with his ophthalmoscope. 'And, of course, my favourite.' He'd scowled at her. 'Drink-driving accidents.'

'I didn't drink anything,' she'd protested. 'Nothing alcoholic, anyway.'

Which was true. Nor had she eaten at the

barbecue either. Maybe if she had she wouldn't be here. It was low blood sugar that had made her sway forward like that, only nobody had listened to her. Then, of course, she'd had to go and wince when they took her pulse.

The corners of her mouth twisted. If only she had eaten something—a mouthful of potato salad, a slice of watermelon. But she hadn't been hungry. Truthfully, she hadn't had much of an appetite for weeks now—

Her thoughts shunted into one another, just as the pick-up had shunted her hours earlier, and in one of those strange distortions of time that kept happening on and off when she wasn't policing her brain she was back in London, reliving those few fraught seconds when she had finally accepted the truth. That happy endings happened to other people. *Not to her.*

She hadn't realised at the time, but that was the moment her marriage—that uncharacteristically optimistic…no, make that *reckless* leap of faith into the unknown—had ended not with a bang, or even a whimper, but a *tut*.

A lump built in her throat, so that it hurt to breathe.

It had been such a tiny sound—the smallest click of tongue against teeth. But it was the smallness of it that had hurt the most. As if that was all she was worthy of. As if that was all he had to give her.

Only she didn't want to think about that now. Actually, she didn't want to think about him—her beautiful, cool-headed, cold-hearted husband—ever.

But, just as in their marriage, what she wanted was irrelevant.

Omar was always there—inside her head. A near-constant presence, jolting her awake from her dreams. Sliding into her thoughts with the same smoothness with which he had once slid into her eager, twitching body.

Heart accelerating, she stared through the gap in the curtains to where he stood on the other side of the ER, his dark head bent over the coffee machine, broad shoulders flexing beneath his blue shirt. She stilled instinctively as the dark head turned towards her. But of course it wasn't Omar. It was just her mind playing tricks on her.

He was miles away, chasing down a deal. He probably hadn't even paused to give a thought to his wife—his soon-to-be ex-wife. Her shoulders stiffened and she felt a twinge of pain—not in her wrist, which was the only part of her injured in the shunt, but in her heart.

It wasn't fair. Over the years she had trained herself to tread lightly through life, not to get attached to anywhere or anyone, and in the past it had never been a problem for her to walk away and keep on walking.

But it had hurt unbearably to leave Omar. As much as if she had cut off an arm. Or a hand. Her gaze dropped to the bare finger on her left hand. The only reason she had managed to do so was because to have stayed would have been an act of wilful self-destruction.

Except it was not that straightforward. As she knew only too well from her parents' very public and much-hyped affair and even more hyped tragic deaths, such acts were like black holes, swallowing those closest and sucking them into the darkness.

Like her father, and Dan, her brothers… She knew how hurt they would be when they found out that her marriage was over.

Angrily, she blanked her mind.

This was her fault. It should be her pain. And, however much it hurt, she was better off right now facing it alone.

And clearly Omar thought so too.

In the days following her leaving she had half thought, half hoped he would come after her. But Omar was no needy man-child like her biological father, Dylan. On the contrary, Omar Al Majid was emphatically, arrogantly male, from the top of his sculpted head to the soles of his handmade shoes and every place in between.

They'd married less than a year ago in Las Vegas. For the briefest, sweetest time he had been her man, and her love for him had been shocking in its intensity. Everything else had retreated. He had been everything.

But almost immediately there had been warning signs. The cut short honeymoon. His laptop always open, its screen glowing day or night because he worked all hours.

Work came first.

Maybe she should have said more, but to have done so would have been to admit how much she loved him, and she still found it hard to be open about her emotions. Like opening Pandora's box, she was both tempted and terrified at the same time. And Omar had always apologised so profusely for the long hours and the working weekends.

Her mouth twisted. He'd had a whole repertoire of apologies.

But after London she'd finally accepted that nothing—certainly no apology—would change the facts. She and Omar had been a real fairy tale—the original, old-fashioned kind, where the Little Mermaid didn't win the heart of her prince but was discarded and turned into sea foam.

She'd had to leave, and the next and the only logical step had been to make things official—which was why she'd filed for divorce a week ago…

Her head snapped up.

Two, maybe three voices, all female, were screaming obscenities. There was a crash of something metallic, followed by the hurried thud of footsteps, and then the curtains parted with a flourish, as if it was the opening night of a Broadway show.

'Hi, Delphi.' It was Carole, frowning over her shoulder as the screaming got louder. 'Sorry about that. Just some Fourth of July family fire-works. How's everything feeling?'

'A bit sore, but basically okay.' As if to test the truth of her words, Delphi moved her wrist from side to side. It hurt a little, but now it was more of a dull ache. 'What time is it?'

'Nearly two.' The nurse smiled. 'Now, as you know, things might be a little painful for a day or two.'

Running her good hand through her short, pinkish blonde pixie cut, Delphi nodded. As the X-rays had shown, it wasn't the first time she'd injured her arm. 'But it's best if you try and keep doing what you normally do. It will speed up the recovery and—'

'So can I leave now?'

Watching the other woman's smile stiffen, she felt like a jerk—and not for the first time.

She wished she had her brothers' easy charm. But she wasn't a people person. It was one of the reasons she had chosen a career working with horses. But this was an ER, so obviously there were lots of people here, and people made her nervous.

Her gaze rested on Carole's face. Logically, she knew it was highly improbable that some nurse at a small hospital in rural Idaho would connect her with that little girl whose face had once been all over the internet. But it was hard to change her behaviour. Difficult to take people at face value. She had learned the hard way that kind words and a smile could distract from all manner of hidden agendas.

Her pulse fluttered. She could still remember the first time Omar had smiled at her. Not just the way it had lit up his face and turned him into a living flame, but also her panicky moth-like response. She had been stunned, disorientated, mesmerised. Torn between wanting to keep on staring at his fascinating curving mouth and a need to turn and run.

She glanced through the gap in the curtains to where the phantom Omar had stood by the coffee machine. It would have been better to run. It was always better—*safer*—to run. And if running wasn't possible, then the next best thing was to keep people at arm's length.

'Yes, you're good to go,' said Carole.

Delphi nodded. 'Thanks.'

Carole gave her the practised smile of a busy nurse. 'You're welcome. Any other questions?'

'Just one.'

Delphi shifted cautiously forward. As her feet touched the floor she stood up, swaying slightly in her high-heeled sandals, the hem of her dress flaring around her ankles.

Earlier, standing at the side of the road, staring at the crumpled back of her car, her first thought, as always, had been to avoid any drama. Drama might lead someone to put two and two together and make four, and before she could blink there would be a whole pack of paparazzi slavering on her doorstep with their long lenses and shouted questions.

That was why she had called her housemate Ashley on the way to the hospital and left a message telling her not to worry, and that she would make her own way back.

Only now she could do without having to wait around for a bus back to Creech Falls.

If this had happened nine months ago she would simply have rung home. Thanks to Omar, that wasn't possible. If she rang home she would have to explain why she was living on her own in Idaho and not in New York with her husband, and it had been agonising enough to admit to herself that her marriage was over.

To admit it to her family would be an entirely new level of pain.

Her heart squeezed with homesickness again, and with love, too, for the man who had adopted her and raised her as his own.

Dan Howard was the best man she knew. He was her pole star, and her brothers, Ed, Scott and Will, made up the compass points that kept her steady and safe. Telling them the truth was going to break their hearts, but particularly her adoptive father's. It was Dan who had introduced Omar to the family. Dan who had encouraged her to trust her instincts and her feelings. To let those feelings show rather than keep them buried.

Her eyes followed the headache-inducing pattern of the curtains from top to bottom. He would be devastated when he found out the truth. That the man he had welcomed as a son had let his adopted daughter down when she'd needed him most. And she would have to break that news to him soon. But not until the bruise around her heart had faded and she could think—no, say Omar's name out loud without stumbling over the syllables. Then at least she might have a chance of persuading Dan that she hadn't been crushed by her selfish, single-minded husband's betrayal.

And, more importantly, convince him that none of this was his fault.

She turned to Carole. 'Do you know if I can pick up a bus to Creech Falls from out front?'

'You can. But you don't need to.' The nurse looked up at her. 'You're getting a lift.'

She was? Delphi frowned. Ashley must have ignored her message. Her throat tightened and she felt a rush of affection for her housemate.

'She didn't need to do that,' she mumbled.

'*She* didn't.' Carole's smile softened as the curtain parted and a man stepped through the gap, his broad, muscular body blocking out the noise and light of the ER.

Every muscle in her body froze. For a few mindless seconds everything including her heartbeat stopped, just as if someone had pressed a pause button. And then, just as swiftly, it began beating double-time.

No, she thought, with a quickening of shock, her eyes still on Carole, feeling herself swaying on her stupid skinny heels. Then, *no*, again, this time more firmly and with a rising panic.

Only some unseen force was turning her head.

And there he was.

Not a mirage or a figment of her imagination but real. Flesh and blood. Bone and muscle. Her husband, Omar Al Majid, in a suit that must have been crafted in some workshop with the sole purpose of advertising the spectacular body that lay beneath.

She stared at him, numb, speechless. A vice was clamping around her ribs. It was all she could do to keep standing upright. She felt weak at the knees. That was the phrase people used, and up until last year she would never have taken it literally. But now here she was, for the second time in her life, shaking inside, her limbs quivering just as they had that very first time she'd seen him at the Amersham Polo Club.

The Amersham was her local club. She had been riding since she was old enough to sit on a horse, and playing polo for almost as long, and Sunday was always match day. Spectators came to enjoy the sunshine and the drama on the field.

She played with her brothers and father. They were a good team and that day they had won their morning match easily. After lunch, she had swapped with Scott and it had been then, standing at the sidelines with the whickering ponies, that she had seen Omar.

Not that she'd known him as Omar then. She hadn't known his name. He was just a man.

An opponent in a dark blue jersey and white breeches. But she hadn't been able to take her eyes off him. And when finally, he'd dismounted his eyes had found hers, just as if he had known exactly where she was.

Feeling his gaze now, she looked up at him, her pulse accelerating. She hadn't been entirely sure when or *if* this moment would ever happen. But she had, of course, acted it out in her head multiple times. What she would say. How Omar would react. Only that didn't stop it being a shock.

But not as much of a shock as the fierce, quivering heat flooding her veins and spilling over her skin, so that for a moment she forgot Carole. Forgot the ache in her arm and the ache in her heart. She forgot everything. She just stood there, drowning in need for him, drinking him in…

Only it was ridiculous to feel that way. To feel anything other than anger for the man standing in front of her. The man who had taken her trust—*no*, demanded it—then casually tossed it in her face. A man who had promised to have her back, to be by her side, only to leave her alone in their penthouse apartment like some forgotten princess in a tower. He might have promised to love and cherish and honour her, but Omar was wedded to his business.

For a split second, her eyes flicked to the man standing in front of her. Over the last six weeks she had been asking herself the same question over and over. Why him? Out of all the men on the planet, why had she given her heart to Omar Al Majid?

Seeing him again, the answer was obvious.

She let her gaze rest on his face.

Typically, overhead fluorescent lighting was harsh and unflattering. Bleaching out colour and warmth and highlighting every tiny flaw and imperfection. But Omar had no flaws or imperfections. Not visible ones, anyway. His beauty was astonishing. Every feature, every angle and line of his face was clean, precise, faceted like a gemstone—and, as with any priceless, glittering jewel, it was impossible to drag your gaze away from it.

Carole clearly felt the same way, she thought, aware suddenly of the nurse's rapt expression. Holding her breath, hating him, hating herself more, she met his gaze.

'Omar.'

'Delphi.'

He spoke softly, but there was a hard gleam in his brown eyes, a tension in the way he was holding his lean muscular body that made her breathing become shallow and her skin grow warm.

'I came as soon as I heard.'

The familiarity of his voice, or rather the dizzying rush of adrenaline it produced, prodded at her already jangling nerves so that for a few moments she didn't take in his actual words, just the smoothness of the syllables. Then she stiffened. What did he mean as soon as he'd heard? Heard how? From whom?

The curtains quivered as a doctor in a white coat strode past, his head lowered over a clipboard.

What had she been thinking? She should never have come here. And she wouldn't have done so. Only the driver of the pick-up—Pete? Was that his name?—had been so upset about hitting her car it had just seemed easier to go along with his insistence.

But, as Dan often said, nothing good came easy.

'How kind,' she said coolly. 'But you really didn't have to go to so much trouble.'

'It was no trouble.'

His mouth—that beautiful mouth that had kissed every centimetre of her body—slanted at one corner like a *fathah* accent.

'I was in San Francisco closing a deal, so it was merely a slight diversion.'

Pain scraped across her skin. *No change there, then*, she thought, a pulse of misery and anger beating in her throat. During the entire time she had known him Omar had always been closing a deal somewhere. It just so happened that today the deal was happening in San Francisco.

'A bit like our marriage,' she said, tilting her chin.

She felt her pulse jerk as his eyes narrowed under the veil of dark lashes, but he didn't react. Instead, he turned his head fractionally to look at Carole. 'Could you give us a moment?'

It was phrased as a question, and if any other man had spoken those exact same words it would have been treated as such. But despite the mildness of his tone there was no mistaking it for anything but an order.

That was how Omar spoke. Who he was.

Omar Al Majid was the son of one of the richest self-made men in the Middle East. His father Rashid's personal wealth was immense, rivalling that of the emirs and sheikhs who ruled the desert lands of the Persian Gulf. In Omar's world—a world which was outside the experience of most normal people—his word was law, his wishes instantly and always satisfied.

Catching sight of the nurse's expression, Delphi felt her pulse start to beat unevenly. It was the same look she had seen countless times on the faces of all those people who'd used to sidle up to her parents in shops and restaurants to ask for selfies or autographs.

It was a mixture of glazed, mute reverence and stunned disbelief that they were in the presence of some near-mythical being. Her stomach twisted. But then, as now, they'd only seen the glittering golden body, not the feet of clay.

'Of course.' The nurse blushed a little and, still staring dazedly up at Omar, disappeared through the curtains.

Now they were alone, his gaze flicked back to her face, and instantly the anger and frustration she had been holding tightly inside for so long surged up inside her. 'What exactly are you doing here, Omar?' she said stiffly.

He was silent for what seemed an eternity, and then he said calmly, 'I would have thought that was obvious.'

There was that same dangerous softness in his voice as before.

'You're hurt, and I'm your husband.'

A shiver ran through her body as he took a step closer.

'Clearly my place is here, by your side.'

Her chin jerked up. 'If you wanted to be by my side, you're about six weeks too late.' The memory of that rainy May morning swelled inside her, and with it an ache that no amount of painkillers could ever numb. 'I needed you then. In fact, I needed you during the nine months of our marriage. I don't need you now.'

Her words were provocative, deliberately so, but Omar didn't so much as blink. He just stood there, watching her in silence, calmly, assessingly.

'You really want to do this now?' he said finally, one smooth, dark eyebrow arching towards the strip lights. 'Here?'

How could he say that so calmly? Stand there with such serenity? But it shouldn't be that much of a surprise. Omar was the master of any social situation—including, it would appear, meeting his estranged wife in an ER at a rural hospital in the middle of Idaho.

'Do what?' Lifting her chin, trying to stay calm or at least look it, she forced herself to hold her gaze steady on his beautiful dark eyes. 'There's nothing left to do. We're done, remember? Finished. Over. Or did you not get the paperwork from my lawyer?'

He frowned. 'It must have got lost.'

She banked down her anger. 'Then I suggest you find it. Or do you think that rocking up here will make me change my mind?'

He did. Even before he spoke she could see it in his eyes. That assumption, so alien to her, that what he wanted to happen would happen.

'We made promises,' he said finally.

Or have you forgotten? She heard his question even though he hadn't asked it, and the tension in her stomach wound tighter. She hadn't forgotten their wedding, but it was easier to remember it when she couldn't see him.

'The kind of promises that mean something…'

He paused, and she thought he was going to say something else, admit that he had let her down, and then a phone rang close by—his phone, she realised a half-second later, and this time there was no pause. She watched in silence, with a pain like hot wire stabbing at her heart, misery and exhaustion swamping her fury as, without missing a beat, he fished it from his pocket and answered it.

'Yeah, that's right… No, send me a transcript and I'll give you a call back with my thoughts.' He ended the call. 'Where was I?'

She gritted her teeth. 'Here. Talking about promises that mean something. But I'm guessing your head is in some boardroom in San Francisco.'

Omar stood for a moment, just looking at her. His face was unreadable, but she could sense his impatience.

'I had to leave a very important meeting to come and find you.' He shook his head. 'But, unlike you, I honour my commitments. Although, given your recent behaviour, it's clear that concept might be beyond you.'

'If you feel that way, I'm surprised you're here. But please don't stay on my account. I'm sure you can find your way out.'

'As usual, you're choosing to misunderstand my intentions. I'm here to help you honour your commitments. Some things can't be left behind. Some things matter too much.'

Was he for real? Delphi stared at him, the hypocrisy of his words making her breathing jerk. Throughout their nine-month marriage, Omar had made it devastatingly clear exactly how important she was to him. Even now, here in the hospital, he was still taking business calls. If they were at home now he would be heading towards his office and she would already be forgotten, swallowed up by the ceaseless hunger of his ambition.

Suddenly it was difficult to look at him, much less speak, and she stared past his shoulder into the crowded ER. 'Yeah, they're really special. It only took you six whole weeks to *rush* to my side.'

His expression didn't alter but his gaze sharpened. 'You're a hard person to find.'

'Apparently not hard enough,' she said tightly. 'And apparently, I'm also not very good at making myself understood. So let me make this completely clear. I don't want anything from you. Except a divorce.'

Silence.

Even the bustle beyond the curtains seemed to still.

Her nerves tightened into a hard knot inside her stomach as he took a step closer.

His fingers cupped her chin. 'But this isn't just about what *you* want, Delphi. The state of matrimony is a partnership. Or it's supposed to be. Only you've spent most of our marriage acting as if you're being corralled against your will.'

She was suddenly aware of the pounding of her heart. In other words it was her fault, not his, that their marriage had faltered.

'Then you'll be glad to be shot of me,' she snapped, jerking her face free of his hand. 'Now, if you wouldn't mind getting out of the way—'

She waited, but he didn't move.

'I do mind.'

His spine straightened, lifting his shoulders and expanding his chest so that his body filled the space between them.

'I just don't know why you do. I'm simply offering you a lift in an air-conditioned limousine. How could you possibly object to that?'

She glared at him. He made it sound as if she

was some diva, turning down a too-small dressing room. But he wasn't the good guy here.

'Easily,' she snapped. Frankly, she'd rather crawl over broken glass than get in a car with Omar. 'I'm happy to take the bus.'

His gaze didn't move from hers. 'They're running a weekend service today. You could be sitting around waiting for hours.'

She stared at him, her skin prickling. 'Oh? And I suppose you know that from your other life as a bus driver?'

'Carole told me.'

His mouth shifted into a shape that made her shiver inside.

'So why not make things easy for yourself?' he asked.

Because nothing good comes easy, she thought again, her heart lurching sideways like a train coming off the rails as his dark eyes locked with hers.

'Because my dad told me never to get into a car with a stranger,' she said hoarsely.

He stared down at her, that mouth of his curving at one corner. 'You're still my wife...' his voice thickened around the word '...my responsibility.'

A wave of misery rose up inside her, blocking her throat. She had so wanted that to be true, and for a time, bathed in the solar intensity of his focus, she had believed it was. She had believed them to be in love—the head-over-heels, truly, madly, deeply kind of love that was as rare and bright as a comet.

But she knew now that what he loved was the chase, and by presenting him with a challenge worthy of some mythical Greek hero she had fuelled his competitive instinct, that same need to win, to call the shots that he displayed both in the boardroom and on the polo field.

And it was why he was here now. She had told him she wanted a divorce, so naturally he had to throw an obstacle in her way.

'I'm not your anything,' she said quickly. 'And, like I told you before, I don't need your help. If I want a lift I can call my housemate, Ashley.'

'Unfortunately not.' He stared down at her through thick dark lashes, his expression unreadable. 'You see, she went to visit her mother. But after she picked up your message she was worried about you. Apparently, you sounded "shaken".'

The pattern of the curtains blurred a little. Ashley had been worried. If things had been different—if Omar had kept his promises—then she might have told him the truth. She might have shared her stomach-churning panic and fear in those few half-seconds when the car had jolted forward.

But he'd let her down so often and so painfully she doubted she would ever trust anyone, again.

'Is there a point to this?' she asked coolly, and saw his expression harden.

'She sent Travis—I think that was his name—to your house to check your passport. See if there was a family member she could get hold of.'

She felt a spike of adrenaline as Omar's mouth did one of those almost-smiles.

'And guess what? I was listed as your next of kin.'

It was a historical mistake to add to the long list of mistakes she'd already made. An oversight. She had meant to cross out his name but forgotten to do so.

'I could call Dan,' he said softly.

She felt as if she might throw up. Her eyes darted to his face.

'Why? So you can play at being the hero?' She shook her head violently. 'That's not going to happen.'

'But you do want to get out of here, don't you?' Without waiting for a reply, he said smoothly, 'Then let me give you a lift.'

Delphi swallowed. Through the curtains she

saw a man limp past on crutches, his foot mummified in bandages, face puffy with bruises. He winced as he moved, but she knew he was leaving the hospital and found herself envying his freedom.

Her heart felt as if it was going to burst through her ribs. She absolutely didn't want to go anywhere with Omar. She certainly didn't want him coming into the untidy little house she shared with Ashley. But she could tell from the set of his shoulders that he wasn't going anywhere without a fight.

Since London the fight had drained out of her, and it was getting harder and harder to balance on her heels. She pressed her leg against the bed to steady herself against a shivering head-rush. Omar was right about one thing. She wanted, *needed* to get out of here—now.

'Okay,' she said curtly. 'You can drive me home. But then I want you gone.'

Not wanting to see the triumph on his face, she turned. The strip-light flickered and the room spun out of focus and her eyes slid sideways, like marbles on a polished floor.

'Delphi?'

His hand closed around her uninjured arm, close to her elbow, guiding her backwards swiftly and purposefully to the bed.

'Here. Sit down.'

She did, shaking off his hand, then choking back a sound that was a mixture of frustration and anger as Omar crouched down in front of her.

He was much too close. Close enough that, had she wanted to, she could have reached out and traced the enviable swell of his biceps beneath the crisp shirt, or pressed her hand against the superbly muscled chest.

'I'm fine,' she muttered, closing her eyes, fighting the urge to lean into his strength. But it was so hard. Hard, too, not to be soothed by the fact that he was there…right there in front of her. Solid. Strong. Steadfast.

Just remember the last time you let your body do the thinking, she told herself. *As for believing in handsome heroes and happy-ever-afters…*

'I'm fine,' she said again, as much for her benefit as his.

'Of course you are.'

In another lifetime, when the vows he'd made were true, that edge to his voice might have been anxiety, but now it was most likely irritation.

'And you were going to go home on your own.'

She sensed rather than saw him shake his head. 'Stay still. I'll get the nurse.'

'No, I just need a moment. And maybe some water.' She let her head tip forward, opening her eyes, focusing on his shoes. 'Could you get me some? There's a water machine somewhere. It'll be quicker than asking someone.'

There was an infinitesimal pause and then her shoulders slumped with relief as he straightened. Slowly she looked up and their eyes met. She held her breath as his dark gaze reached inside her, considering her request and his response.

'Just don't move,' he ordered. 'I'll be right back.'

She wanted to tell him not to bother, but instead she watched, her pulse skipping as he strode away.

Five minutes later Omar snapped back the curtain, a bottle of water in his hand.

'Here. Drink this. I've—'

He stopped mid-sentence, his pupils flaring with shock and incredulity.

The bed was empty.

Delphi was gone.

CHAPTER TWO

OMAR LIFTED A hand and pressed two fingers against his right temple, where his head was starting to pound. His brain, usually so quick and decisive, was struggling to accept what his eyes were showing him.

But maybe he was jumping the gun and she had simply gone outside to get some fresh air.

Turning, he flicked the curtain aside and stalked back across the ER, his eyes scanning the room *Terminator*-style, looking for a flash of rose-pink among all the blue scrubs.

But with every step he took he knew he was wasting his time. Like the horses she worked with, running away was Delphi's default response to any kind of confrontation or threat. Especially when she was angry, and she was still angry with him. Still blamed him for what had happened in London. Hence the divorce papers.

He rubbed his fingers against his forehead, trying to relieve the pressure.

Except nothing had actually happened. Okay, it had been upsetting that the paparazzi were hanging around, and frustrating that she hadn't been able to visit her parents' graves, but her reaction had felt—*still* felt—disproportionate. Unreasonable. Unfair.

He'd known Delphi was angry with him for not going to England with her, but he had apologised multiple times. In fact, he seemed to have spent half his married life apologising to Delphi.

And how would it have changed anything even if he had gone with her?

What was more, she had never once admitted the part *she'd* played. If she had stuck to the original plan he would have been by her side. But she had changed her mind not once but twice about going to London, and by then he'd been offered a meeting with Bob Maclean, owner of the biggest cable network in North America.

A meeting like that was not something he could just postpone, and he had tried to explain that to Delphi. But nothing he'd said had consoled her. She had simply blocked each attempt he'd made, silently retreating further and further into herself, so that once again she had become that guarded young woman he had met at the polo a year ago.

His jaw tightened. With hindsight he should have refused to accept her silence. When she had frozen him out in London he should have sat her down and made her talk. Or just taken her to bed and kept her there until the ice had melted.

Maybe if he had they would be in a different place now.

Or maybe they wouldn't, he thought as he strode towards the exit.

He was well past the point of thinking their marriage could be fixed. Although, as he'd walked into the hospital, a part of him had wondered if she'd had time to think and perhaps regret her actions.

She hadn't, of course.

Delphi was the most stubborn person he had ever met. And the hardest to pin down.

Apart from Rashid Al Majid.

The doors slid open, and as he walked purposefully into the warm Idaho sunlight he glanced upwards at a sky that was the same faded blue as his father's eyes. Eyes that were always tracking away from him, seeking something brighter, bigger, shinier—

His shoulders tensed. With sixteen older half-siblings, it was almost impossible for him to offer anything new, anything special or standout that might snag Rashid's attention. But that hadn't stopped him from trying. On the contrary, he had spent most of his life striving to form a bond with his elusive, uncompromising father by building something he could call his own, something that had nothing to do with his family.

Two birds, one stone. Twin goals. Inseparable and inexorable. Consummate and constant.

But as for marriage…

He had considered it. It had always been more of an assumption that he would marry at some point than an ambition.

Until he'd met Delphi.

And then it had become an obsession. Getting her to trust him had become the plan that had driven everything else from his mind. It had taken the best part of three months to succeed, but he'd done it.

The band of silver on his left hand glinted in the sunlight.

Or rather he'd thought he had. Only apparently, according to Delphi's ridiculously high and ever-upward-moving bar, he had failed.

Failed.

The word scraped against his skin, drawing blood.

Except this wasn't *his* failure. He had gone

above and beyond what any other man would have done to prove himself worthy. He had accepted her past unquestioningly, even though it had raised eyebrows among the more conservative members of his family. And not once had he considered walking away.

But one tiny mistake on his part—more of a misstep, really—and Delphi had bailed on him, on their marriage. Just packed her bags and left. Exactly as her mother had done to Dan.

Only instead of taking fourteen years, it had taken her just shy of nine months.

Eyes narrowing, he stared at the Delphi-free queue of people waiting to be picked up.

At first, he'd thought she just needed time to cool off, and he'd assumed that she would go home to Bedford—to the ranch. But she hadn't. As he'd found out when Dan had called the next day and it had become obvious that Delphi was not with her family and nor had she told them about the row.

He felt a flicker of exasperation. That was all he'd thought it was then. *A row.* Although 'row' made it sound as if they had shouted at each other, when in reality Delphi had said so little it hardly constituted a conversation, let alone an argument.

It hadn't occurred to him that he was witnessing the last gasp of their marriage.

His mouth twisted. For most of their relationship Delphi had made him feel as if he was cross-examining her in the witness box. Everything had to be coaxed out of her, and even then she held things back. But she had been ruthless about ending things between them. Having made her decision unilaterally, she had left.

Walking into their empty apartment, he had felt stricken, shocked, and her absence had been made all the more devastating by the sudden rush of memories it had provoked of coming home as a child to find his father gone.

But as the days had passed and it had become clear that Delphi was gone for good, his shock and misery had been consumed by a black, all-consuming rage that she could just walk away and move on with her life without him.

Not that he would have had her back. He was done with it. With her. With her stubborn refusal to talk, to share herself with him. What was the point of being married to someone who felt like that?

No, divorce was the only option. His one regret was that he couldn't serve her with the papers first.

But he was not done with his errant wife just yet.

Glancing again at the queue of people, he felt his stomach twist. It was pure coincidence that he had been so close geographically when that cowboy had called him and told him Delphi was in hospital. Pure chance he had even picked up the call.

It had been an unknown number. Ordinarily he would have let it ring out, go to messages, but something—some sixth sense, maybe—had moved him to answer.

The knot in his stomach tightened painfully. It was impossible to give a name to the tangle of emotions he'd felt as he'd walked into the hospital just under an hour ago and seen Delphi sitting on the bed talking to some doctor. Exasperation. Disbelief. Relief that he had finally found her and that her injuries were minor.

Only now she was gone again. And his relief was long gone too, swallowed up by a hot, pulsing fury that she had done it again. She had walked out of his life. Sneaked off when his back was turned.

His jaw clenched.

But surely someone must have seen something? he thought irritably, glancing over to where a man on crutches was now joining the end of the queue. In that dress and those heels Delphi was hardly invisible. Remembering how the fabric had flared over the curves of her bottom, he felt heat pulse across his skin, accompanied by a little drumroll of jealousy.

She never wore dresses or heels. So why was she now? And where was her wedding ring?

The pale indentation on her finger had taunted him. Had she already found someone else? Was running away from the promises she'd made not the only thing she had in common with her mother?

He pictured a man holding Delphi's ringless hand, wrapping his arm around her waist as he pulled her closer. Had she replaced him already?

A rush of fury—male, possessive, visceral—pushed everything else from his mind, so all that remained was a savage, mindless urge to find whoever he was and batter him into the ground.

Was that why she was so eager to get a divorce?

Back inside the hospital, he had lied to Delphi. He had, of course, seen the papers sent by her lawyers, but even just thinking about them made the pounding inside his skull ramp up a notch. And not just because it stung, imagining himself being so easily and swiftly replaced.

Being the first person in his family to get divorced was not what he'd had in mind when he'd dreamed of doing something unique… something that would grab his father's attention. But he was done with trying to make his marriage work. He couldn't—not on his own. And he was on his own. It had just taken her leaving for him to realise that.

He wanted this divorce as much as she did—maybe even more. But right now, she was still his wife, and she had one more task to perform before he dismissed her, and she became nothing more than a faint crease pressed into a single page of his life.

Jaw clenching, he walked to the beginning of the meandering queue.

'Excuse me…' He smiled stiffly at a woman with her foot in a cast. 'I'm looking for my wife. I was supposed to meet her out here. I don't suppose you've seen her. She's about so high.' He raised his hand to just below his shoulder. 'Short pinkish blonde hair. Wearing a white dress.'

The woman nodded. 'She went that way,' she said, pointing over Omar's shoulder, and then she frowned. 'But she didn't look like she was waiting for nobody. In fact, she seemed in kind of a hurry.'

Of course she was, Omar thought, striding swiftly away from the hospital.

'That way' turned out to be on to a Main Street straight out of a theme park. There were a couple of banks and some small, shabby-looking shops, all closed for the holiday, and a barber's, also closed. In both the two restaurants staff were wiping down the tables. He scanned the street. Everywhere was either shut or closing up for the day.

Every place except one.

Dark eyes narrowing, Omar crossed the road.

Sliding into a booth in the corner of the Iron Mule Tavern, Delphi breathed out shakily. She had virtually sprinted away from the hospital, and now her lungs were burning and the ache in her wrist had returned.

She hadn't planned to run. Or maybe she had subconsciously. Because that had been the first thought that had popped into her head when Omar strode away.

Run. Run as fast as you can.

And she had. Blindly, unthinkingly, like an animal seeking a place to hide from a predator. And now, thankfully, she was safe. She could stop running, relax. Celebrate, even. Her own personal day of independence. Except she didn't feel much like celebrating.

Clearly she had come to the right place, she thought, glancing across the room to where a barmaid was standing listlessly behind a sticky-looking counter. Opposite her sat six men, all old, hunched over their glasses, eyes glued to the television mounted on the wall. None of them had even looked over when she'd walked in, which was just the way she liked it.

'What can I get you?'

The barmaid had made her way over and was standing next to the table, a bored expression on her face.

'Vodka, please,' Delphi said quickly.

Behind them, the door to the bar banged open and she jerked round, her body humming with panic. But it was just another old man, with sparse straw-coloured hair and vein-hatched cheeks.

She swallowed. 'Make it a double.'

The barmaid nodded, still bored.

Watching her walk away, Delphi leaned back against the faux leather, her body buckling. She needed something a lot stronger than water to blunt the emotions raging inside her. And not just because of Omar's sudden unwelcome reappearance in her life.

Throat tightening, she moved her hand protectively to her wrist. It was such a stupid thing to have let happen, and it shouldn't have happened. Like everybody else in her family she was a careful driver, never taking risks or cutting corners. Because, like them, she understood the consequences could be devastating.

Fatal.

Her breath caught as it always did when she thought about the accident.

To her, Ianthe Reynolds and Dylan Wright had just been Mummy and Daddy. But to the rest of the world the peroxide blonde actress and the pouting up-and-coming pop star had been an 'it' couple. Their affair had been chronicled with voyeuristic frenzy in the tabloids, starting when Ianthe had left Dan Howard, her husband of fourteen years, for her much younger lover, and ending when the car Ianthe had been driving had spun off the road, killing them both.

And just like that Delphi had become an orphan.

She was four years old.

It would be wrong to say that she could remember those first few hours after the crash. Mostly what she remembered was just a blur of people coming in and out of the house. And lights…lots of flashing lights.

The door to the bar banged open again. This time she didn't turn her head. She couldn't look away from the lights in her memory. Red and blue for the police. Then, later, white for the *paparazzi*, who had joined the TV camera crews treading on the fragile heads of the tulips she and her father had planted in December. She could still hear their voices, seeping through the walls and echoing down the pipes…still picture their faces flushed with greedy excitement.

A shiver ran over her skin and she felt an almost imperceptible change in air pressure, like the tremble of debris at the mouth of a subway tunnel before a train arrived. And then—

'There you are, darling.'

She jumped as a bottle of water was slammed down onto the table.

'Sorry it took so long. I didn't realise we were playing hide and seek. *Again*.'

Delphi felt her stomach drop. Her heart squeezed as if she was having a seizure. Looking as out of place in the dusty bar as a peacock in a pigeon loft, Omar Al Majid was staring down at her, his beautiful sexy mouth set in a grim line.

'But I suppose I should have guessed. It *is* your favourite game.'

Her pulse scuttled. He had been angry before, but now she could almost see the fury and frustration shimmering around his body like a heat haze in the desert. But he could be as angry as he liked. It wouldn't change anything. Certainly not the past. Or the future. And after what had happened in London she knew they had no future.

Her fingers moved to her stomach and she felt something pinch inside her—that same pang of regret and loss that punctuated her day like a clock marking the hours.

She lifted her chin and met his gaze. 'I don't play games. Don't sit down,' she snapped.

But it was too late. Omar had already dropped into the seat opposite her, stretching out his long legs so that she would have to climb over him to make her escape.

'No, you just sneak away when no one's around.'

He pushed the bottle of water towards her across the table. She stopped it with her hand.

'I didn't sneak anywhere. I didn't want to see you.'

'Or you send them on a fool's errand,' he continued, ignoring her remark.

'If the cap fits...' she said coolly.

A muscle twitched in his cheek, and he jerked his hand away from the bottle.

She felt a flicker of triumph, but it was swiftly extinguished as he leaned back in his seat and her eyes felt suddenly as if they were on the end of a fishing hook, reeled in inexorably by the tightening of fabric around smooth, toned muscle.

He looked good in a suit. Good out of one too, she conceded, her breath quickening as, against her will, she found herself remembering every centimetre of his superb body in glorious detail.

As if he could read her thoughts, Omar looked at her across the sticky table.

'It doesn't.' His gaze was steady and unwavering. 'You see, you don't fool me, Delphi. How could you? I mean, you can't even fool yourself.'

Suddenly she was fighting the wild beating of her heart. 'I don't know what you're talking about,' she said stiffly, her fingers thick and clumsy around the neck of the bottle.

But she did. She could feel it now, one beat behind her pulse. A longing that had nothing to do with logic. A need that was like an itch beneath the skin. Impossible to scratch no matter how much you twisted and squirmed.

A slow smile tugged at the corners of his mouth and the table seemed to shrink. Around them the bar lost shape, the hunched drinkers and the barmaid blurring into one another so that there was just her and him. Omar Al Majid, the man with eyes that could hold her fast in a hurricane.

'Sure you do.' He dismissed her statement with a careless lift of his broad shoulders. 'You just have trouble admitting it. You always have. That's why you ran away, and why you're hiding in some downtown bar in a two-bit town. But there are some truths you can't run from.'

She shivered all the way through, the air leaving her body as he leaned forward. And she wanted to run then—run from the dark heat in his gaze and from the memory of his body flexing beneath hers as he held her waist and thrust up into her—

Breathing in sharply, she pressed her legs together beneath the table, trying to deny the pulse beating between her thighs. How could she feel like this? After everything he had done and failed to do, it was crazy of her body to behave this way—not to say treacherous.

Then again, what did all this heat and twitchiness amount to? It was just sex. Bodies. Biology.

Legally, Omar might still be her husband, but their marriage was null and void. Anything else was just wishful thinking on her part. A stupid, irrational hope that she could outrun her past, outrun the twisting helix of her DNA. Only how could you ever outrun something that was a part of you?

And it was all immaterial now, anyway. She was over him. *Clearly.* Why else would she file for divorce? It was so she could be free of him…free to get on with her life.

'I'm not running. I'm sitting down, waiting

for my drink to arrive so I can celebrate my imminent independence from you. But why wait?' She snatched up the bottle of water and twisted off the top. 'Here's to single life.'

The cold water burned her throat as his beautiful eyes narrowed. 'I know what you're trying to do, Delphi. I wonder, though, do you?'

She could feel her pulse thudding beneath the thin fabric of her dress. 'It's really not that complicated, Omar. I'm trying to get you to leave.'

He stared across the table, that mouth of his curving into a smile that sliced through her skin. 'Exactly. You're needling me because there's nowhere left to run, nowhere left to hide, and you're scared.'

'I'm not scared of you.'

She spoke quickly—too quickly.

'No, you're scared of *us*. You're scared of what "us" means, and how it makes you feel. How *I* make you feel.' His eyes shifted pointedly to the dull white of her knuckles, where her hand was clamped to the bottle. 'It's what's always scared you, right from the start. And I know that when it gets too much you do what you did six weeks ago…what you're doing now. Instead of talking to me, you push me away. You run. You retreat. You overreact.'

Overreact.

Delphi stared at him in silence, the word

knocking the breath from her lungs. Back in the hospital, when he had stepped into the cubicle, she had actually thought things might be different. *He* might be different. But nothing had changed. Instead of understanding that her actions had originated out of a need to survive, he saw only a challenge.

But this wasn't about her pushing him away. It was about self-preservation. It was about her trusting him, and him letting her down. Repeatedly. Day in, day out. Every day a little piece of her had been chipped away. That was why she had left. Because if she'd stayed there would have been nothing left of her.

Only he had no idea of what he'd done. Actually, he didn't think he had done anything. As far as Omar was concerned, she was the one at fault. She was the one who had reacted—*overreacted.*

Still blindsided by the injustice of that word, she shook her head. 'And that's why you think I left? Because I'm scared of how being with you makes me feel?' She resisted the impulse to slap his stupidly handsome face. He really was the most monumentally arrogant and selfish man on the planet. 'Do you know what your problem is, Omar?'

He raised an eyebrow questioningly, as if he hadn't until now considered the possibility that he might possess one. Probably he hadn't. For men like Omar, other people were always to blame.

'You're so busy building your empire, so obsessed with whatever deal it is you're making, you don't ever stop and take a look at yourself. At who *you* are. And how *you* behave.'

'How I behave?' A muscle tightened in his jaw. 'I'm not the one who walked out on our marriage without so much as a word of explanation.'

She felt her pulse jerk. Would explaining have changed anything? Perhaps in that moment, yes. Omar would have been devastated to know that she had been pregnant and lost the baby.

There was a heavy feeling at the back of her eyes as she remembered her breathless shock, the hot, wet stickiness of her blood. Yes, he would have been devastated—but then what? People didn't change—not really, and not for very long. The miscarriage had simply made her face up to the fact that she came and would always come second to his work.

The part of her that had still been hoping for a happy ending had slipped away in that bathroom too. Lying on the cold tiles, she had accepted that there was something wrong with her. Something that meant that a happy ending would always be out of reach.

So Omar was right. There were some truths you couldn't hide from. They were just talking about different truths.

'We shared a bed and a ceremony,' she said flatly. 'But it takes more than a ring and piece of paper to make a marriage.'

Omar stared down at Delphi's bare fingers, anger and outrage rippling over his skin in waves. Did she really, seriously think *she* could lecture *him* about what made a marriage?

With an effort of will, he held his breath, hung on to his temper. He would deal with the ring later…

'It's not just a piece of paper. It's a legally binding contract.'

She held his gaze. 'So is divorce.'

He gritted his teeth, wanting to shake her. She had no idea what he'd been through these past weeks. Nor, apparently, did she care, he thought, his gaze searching and failing to find any evidence of remorse in her clear brown eyes. But if she thought she could just toss their marriage away like a broken toy, she was going to be in for a nasty surprise.

Almost as nasty as coming home and finding your wife gone.

'Marriage isn't just about the individual and the personal, Delphi. You have obligations to meet, liabilities owed.'

She gave a bitter laugh. 'Trust you to see marriage as a balance sheet.'

Her words stung. And what had she seen it as? A gamble? A chance to reinvent herself. A trap? He didn't like the tightness in the chest those thoughts provoked.

'But you didn't, did you?' he said slowly. 'Trust me, I mean.'

She stilled like a small animal trapped in the beam of a poacher's torch. For a moment she looked young, even younger than she was, vulnerable, almost fragile, and remembering the accident he felt a stab of guilt. But then his mood hardened as her expression hardened into a scowl.

'Wisely, as it turned out,' she said.

'Here you go.'

Their heads snapped round as one.

The barmaid was back.

He watched, his pulse drumming irritably, as she slid a glass onto the table. Opposite him, Delphi sat stiffly, angled off the seat, one foot arched upwards like a sprinter. Preparing to run again, he thought. Although those spike-heeled sandals were hardly designed for running. More for showcasing her legs.

Not that he needed reminding. He knew every inch of them intimately. A beat of heat skimmed over his skin. And how it felt when she wrapped them around his hips…

Delphi leaned forward, shoulders braced, and then her chin tilted upwards, and he realised that he had been wrong. She wasn't poised to run. She was waiting to dismiss him. Just like his father had done so many times in his life.

As if on cue, his phone vibrated in his pocket. He reached for it automatically, his pulse accelerating as he scrolled down to read the email. He felt a tick of satisfaction. It was a good deal. He would talk to the lawyers, tie up the loose ends, and then maybe call Rashid.

Sliding his phone back into his jacket, he looked up to find Delphi staring at him, her face still and set.

'What is that?' he asked as she picked up the glass.

'Vodka,' she said crisply.

He held her gaze. 'I don't think drinking alcohol after an accident is a good idea.'

She shrugged. 'Your time would be better spent getting used to the idea that what you think, say or do is no longer any of my concern.'

There was a short, hard pause, and then she downed her drink in one.

Tamping down a sharp, unprecedented urge to haul her across the table and prove her wrong by pressing her body against his and his mouth to hers, he switched his gaze across the room to the TV screen, where two wrestlers in figure-hugging shorts and lace-up boots were throwing each other around a ring to the cheers of an enthusiastic crowd.

He stared at the screen, his teeth on edge, body taut. It was a performance, of course. But the effort it took to plan those moves and the skill required to execute them with panache was real in the same way that his parents' marriage was real. Rashid and Maryam hadn't married for love, but they had worked their way to affection and understanding. Theirs was a commitment based on pragmatism. A strategic, choreographed performance by two invested participants.

He respected that, but he had never wanted it for himself. Until this moment, when it seemed infinitely preferable to this impasse of a marriage he shared with Delphi.

He studied her profile: the small straight nose, the high arched cheekbones, the soft mouth. Back at the hospital he'd wanted to give her a chance to do the right thing, but she had thrown it back in his face. So now they would do things his way.

'My time would be better spent anywhere but here.' He got to his feet. 'Let's go.'

Her eyes narrowed. 'For the last time, I'm not going anywhere with you.'

'You will. Either on your own two feet or over my shoulder. You choose.'

She gave him an icy, disbelieving glare. 'You wouldn't dare.'

'Try me,' he said coolly.

He was calling her bluff. But, as the daughter of Ianthe Reynolds and Dylan Wright, he knew she'd blink first. She hated fuss, drama, scenes of any kind, and he felt a stab of satisfaction as Delphi got to her feet and sidestepped past him.

Outside, he lifted his hand in an imperious gesture. Instantly an SUV appeared round the corner and pulled up alongside the kerb.

'You've stopped fighting me,' he said as he joined her in the back seat and the car began to move smoothly forward.

'I don't need to fight you anymore.' She shifted sideways, pressing her body against the door. 'It will only take thirty minutes to get back home. And then you'll be out of my life for good. Back to San Francisco, or wherever your next mega deal is taking place.'

'I'm not going to San Francisco.'

He stretched his legs, dragging out the moment, wanting to prolong the sensation of having her right where he wanted her. Just like he had in bed.

'I'm going to Dubai. And if you want a divorce—a nice, quick, uncomplicated divorce...' He paused, his eyes finding hers. 'Then you will be coming with me. As my wife.'

There was a small, stunned pause. In the subdued light of the car he could see her fighting to stay calm.

'If you think that's going to happen then maybe we should go back to the hospital and get *you* examined by a doctor.'

Her voice was steady, but the tick of fury beneath it tugged at his senses. She was close to losing control.

'What part of *I want a divorce* don't you understand, Omar?'

'What part of *We're still married* don't you?' he shot back. 'And we *are* still married, Delphi.' Reaching over, he caught her hand, turning it knuckle-side up. 'With or without a ring. For better *and* worse.'

Her nostrils flared as she struggled to pull her hand away. 'You can say that again.' Twisting her fingers, she made a sound of frustration. 'Why are you doing this? I know you have to win, but I'm not one of your business deals.'

'Indeed you are not.' His eyes meshed with

hers. 'In comparison to our marriage, any business deal would be a walk in the park.'

'Then why can't you just let me leave?'

He gritted his teeth, his body tensing, on edge. 'Because you, my sweet, selfish wife, made promises. One of which was to attend my father's ninetieth birthday party.'

That got to her, he thought as her eyes widened.

He released his grip. 'Perhaps in your quest for independence that slipped your mind. But it hasn't slipped mine.'

And he was prepared to exploit the chemistry she was so desperate to deny one last time to get what he wanted.

When the car stopped, he got out. Seconds later, as he had known he would, he heard a door slam. The click of heels.

'What you're asking is impossible.'

He turned. Delphi was standing in front of him. A light breeze tugged at her dress so that it clung to her legs, and he felt a current of hunger curl beneath his anger.

'For you to attend an event as my wife?' He frowned. 'How so? It's not something you haven't done before.'

He saw her hands ball into fists.

'Being a wife isn't just a title It's what you feel about a person. I don't feel that way about you.'

Her face was back to that carefully schooled mask he knew so well.

'I'm not an actress. You can't just snap your fingers and ask me to perform.'

Later he would wonder if it was that click of her fingers or the cool, maddening indifference of her expression that made him step forward. But in that moment, he had no conscious thought. He was just pure need.

'I'm not asking.'

In one seamless movement he grabbed her shoulders and yanked her against him. He fitted his mouth to hers, claiming her as he had done a thousand times before and would have done a thousand times more if she hadn't walked out on their marriage.

He felt her tense, her hands pressing into his chest, pushing, and then not pushing but pulling him closer.

He heard her breathing quicken and felt a spike of satisfaction as she leaned into him, her fingers clutching at his jacket.

She might be able to hide everything else, but in his arms she couldn't hide the need she felt. A need that mirrored and matched his own.

Hunger and heat swamped him. It burned everything in its path, consuming the past, melting the present.

Her lips were soft and urgent, her tongue was

in his mouth, his in hers, their hands were in each other's hair, tugging, teasing, not tender but frantic, unthinking, ungovernable, astonishingly carnal.

It was not enough.

Behind him, across the fields came a distant flurry of thunder. No, not thunder. Fireworks.

He dragged his mouth from hers. She stepped backwards, stumbling a little, her hands clenching. She looked like he felt. Shaking inside, shaken by the burst of heat that was still roaring through him.

He forced himself to meet her gaze. 'See,' he said softly. 'I didn't even need to click my fingers.'

Her pupils flared. 'I don't have my passport.'

'But I do.' He reached into his jacket and pulled it out. 'I had one of my people pick it up this morning. So, if there's nothing more, I suggest we get going. We're on a tight schedule as it is.'

And, ignoring both the flames still crackling through his body and her pale, trembling face, he turned and walked across the runway to the waiting plane.

CHAPTER THREE

EXACTLY FOURTEEN HOURS and nine minutes after it took off from the runway in Idaho, Omar's Gulfstream jet landed in Dubai with an almost imperceptible shudder.

As it taxied smoothly up the runway, Delphi gazed out of the window at a sky that was darkening as she watched. She wasn't a nervous flyer, but her fingers trembled against the magazine she had been pretending to read for the last hour of the flight.

Obviously she had known this moment was going to happen. The plane couldn't keep circling the skies for ever. But now it was here, and the real-time consequences of what she had agreed to back in the States were no longer a distant possibility but an unavoidable certainty.

Not that there was any paperwork, she thought. It was more of a non-verbal agreement.

Remembering those few febrile half-seconds when she and Omar had kissed, she felt her face grow warm. Except it had been less a kiss and more a forced admission of a need that shouldn't still exist, yet inexplicably did.

Glancing down the cabin to where Omar was sitting, his dark head bent over the screen of his laptop, she felt her pulse stumble. In his arms, time had not just stopped, but reversed. Everything had turned to air—her anger, his frustration, all of it—and there had been just the two of them in the moment, tearing at each other's clothes.

It had been fierce and thorough. A rolling and impossible longing and a banked, devastating desire.

And then he had pulled away, and it had been like jerking awake from a vivid dream to find yourself asleep in front of the TV. One moment he'd been kissing her, all seductive heat and wild longing, the next he'd been discussing their flight schedule.

It had been in that moment, with his dark eyes moving restlessly across the sun-soaked Idaho fields and the aftershocks of his kiss still pounding through her body like a herd of stampeding mustang, that she'd understood why Omar had kissed her and why he had stopped.

Whatever it had felt like, it had had nothing to do with desire and everything to do with winning. Like a sniper choosing a rifle, he had weaponised their unfinished physical attraction for one another, recognising it as the simplest, most expedient way for him to silence her opposition. Figuratively and literally.

As if he sensed the path of her thoughts, Omar looked up from across the cabin, and with agonising slowness she turned to stare out of the window. Other than a few stiffly polite conversations when the cabin crew were present, they had barely spoken during the flight, and she was dreading having to play the role of his wife more convincingly at the party.

She swallowed—tried to, anyway. Only her throat was suddenly dry, tight.

Her hands gripped the armrests. Maybe she could just refuse to get off the plane. Like a kind of reverse hostage. Only she knew she wouldn't. And not only because Omar would probably just hoist her over his shoulder and carry her off, kicking and screaming. The truth was that even though she had only met Rashid once before, she felt bad about forgetting his birthday party. It wasn't his fault that his son had let her down. Or that his birthday had coincided with their marriage imploding.

She glanced furtively over to where Omar was talking to the air stewards.

What were they thinking? Did they wonder

why she was sitting at the other end of the plane from her husband?

Her gaze shifted minutely to his open laptop. Not if they had spent any amount of time with their boss, she thought. They would know that work came before everything, including his wife.

Her eyes rested on his back. He had changed clothes during the flight. Now, instead of a suit, he was wearing faded blue jeans and a black T-shirt, just like most of the men who worked at the stables.

Although it was highly improbable that anyone would ever confuse Omar with a groom. You could put an ordinary general-purpose saddle on a thoroughbred, but it wouldn't stop it being a racehorse, and even in the most casual of clothing Omar radiated an aura of power and the kind of absolute self-assurance that made waiters scuttle across restaurants and women blush and bite their lip.

She bit her own lip, then released it quickly, shoulders tensing against the leather upholstery. It made no sense to look down on the rest of the population for reacting that way. Not when she was just as susceptible as everyone else, leaning into him like a moth helplessly pulled to the light.

At least she wasn't kidding herself anymore

that it was some fairy tale fantasy of love. And it *had* been a fairy tale, thinking that she could fall in love and be loved and have her happy ever after.

Some happy-ever-after! They hadn't even made it to their first wedding anniversary.

Watching him sleep, the morning after their wedding, she had felt her love for him like a superpower. It had crackled beneath her skin like electricity, and she had wanted to drag him back to the chapel and make new promises, to go into battle for him, for their marriage.

But months of always coming second to his work had taken its toll. After London, it had been as if some internal energy grid had shut down. She had waited until he went to work one day, packed a small bag, and left.

She leaned her head back against the seat. Occasionally, when she could longer fight it and the pain threatened to overwhelm her, she told herself that having your heart broken was a rite of passage and that it was a 'good' pain.

Her gaze snagged on Omar's flawless profile.

It wasn't!

She glanced away. But there was no point in thinking about any of that. She couldn't change the past. All she could do was learn from her mistakes. At least that way she could make those mistakes have some value. Her heart began beating a little faster. Although she wasn't entirely sure how coming to Dubai as Omar's wife fitted in with that philosophy…

'Everything okay?'

Her pulse skipped like a startled rabbit. Omar was standing beside her with the light behind him, his eyes soft and almost black.

No, she thought, and briefly revisited the idea of refusing to leave.

But instead, she undid her seatbelt and got to her feet. 'Yes.' She nodded.

'Good,' he said coolly.

He stared down at her. For a moment she thought he was going to take her hand, or perhaps her arm, and she was suddenly and acutely conscious of the rise and fall of her breath. But he didn't move.

She felt her belly clench, the muscles quivering. He didn't need to. He never had. Just being close to him made her feel hot and tight and restless, as if she had been out in the sun too long.

'Shall we get this over and done with?' she said abruptly.

She got to her feet and, stepping outside, stared dazedly at the glowing orange sun sinking beneath the horizon. Right about now in Creech Falls she would have been rubbing sleep from her eyes and rolling out of bed, and her body was still working on Pacific Standard Time. But that wasn't what made her steady herself against the handrail.

It had been hot in Idaho, but this was like stepping into a solid wall of heat. It was a tangible force that pushed back against her body, then swallowed her up. She could already feel her light cotton blouse sticking to her skin.

'It gets a lot hotter during the day. You'll need to take care outside.'

Omar was standing beside her. In the final flickering rays of the sun he looked like a bronze statue of some desert warrior king, not sweating, but shimmering in the heat.

Instantly, she felt hotter and stickier, and grumpier. 'Sweet of you to worry,' she said, focusing her temper on his handsome face. 'But I don't think it will be a problem. I'm sure they'll have sun canopies at the hotel.'

Omar had told her that she would be staying at the Lulua and, having looked it up on the flight, she knew that all the jaw-droppingly expensive suites there came with their own private terrace and infinity pool, so there would be no reason to leave.

He stared at her in silence meditatively. Then, 'If you say so.' He gestured to the steps. 'After you.'

On the runway below a limousine was parked between three SUVs, all with blacked-out windows. Four men wearing dark suits and traditional *ghutras* stood next to the driver's door of each car. Two other men, each roughly the size of a professional wrestler, waited on either side of the limousine, scanning the empty runway with thousand-yard stares.

She stilled, her body stiffening like an animal sensing a trap. She had grown up surrounded by wealth, but security at her father's estate had been low-key. In New York, Omar preferred a more obvious presence. But this felt almost theatrically excessive.

'My father sent them,' Omar said quietly. 'I know it feels a little over the top, but it's just how he likes things done.'

Which, roughly translated, meant that the wishes of Rashid Al Majid would prevail one way or another. *Like father like son*, she thought as they walked across the runway to the waiting cars.

Thankfully, the limousine was blissfully cool after the furnace heat outside. Omar leaned forward and said something in Arabic to the driver, and even though her nerves were still jangling with jet lag and panic she found herself admiring the way he could switch so effortlessly between languages. After a summer living and working at a polo stud in Argentina she could speak some Spanish, but nowhere near as well as Omar. And he spoke other languages too. For business reasons, he'd told her.

Her mouth thinned. What other reason could there be?

Most people worked to live. Omar lived to work. It consumed him. Even when he wasn't working, which wasn't often, some part of him was always thinking about work. No doubt in his dreams, he pursued CEOs across desk-strewn office landscapes in the same way the dogs on the ranch chased imaginary rabbits in their sleep.

Her dreams were different. Confused and confusing so that when she woke, she felt more anxious, less certain. She thought back to when she'd been deciding whether to go and visit her parents' graves. It had been her first visit to England since their funerals, and in the past she had always found a reason to stay away. It hadn't been hard: there were so many. And it had been the same this time—only then she'd discovered she was pregnant, and it had seemed like a sign. A chance to reconcile the past with a future she had never imagined having.

A flash of headlights on the side of the carriageway made her blink. She hadn't told Omar she was pregnant. He had been away on business but it had still been a big decision to visit the graves. Omar had known that, and he had told her repeatedly that he would support her, be by her side. He had asked her to trust him—no, *demanded* that she trust him, and she had. Idiot that she was, she had believed he would be there for her.

But when it had come to it, his work came first. It always came first. She was just a diversion.

It had been the end of the beginning.

What had followed was the beginning of the end.

'That's the Burj Khalifa.'

Omar's voice cut across the quiet murmur of the engine and the less quiet clamour of her thoughts and she glanced out of the window. She wasn't generally that bothered about buildings. There was so much in the natural world to astonish. But now she stared in stunned silence at the illuminated needle-thin spire of metal that seemed to pierce the dark blue sky, almost touching the stars.

'Wow,' she said softly. 'It's like something out of *Brave New World*.'

Omar's dark eyes rested on her face. 'I suppose there is something courageous about taking on the desert.'

That was one word for it.

Tilting her head, she stared up at the Burj, not really seeing the glittering tower anymore. Instead, the lit-up windows reminded her of the keyboard on Omar's laptop when she used to wake in bed and find him working in the darkness.

He wasn't a builder, or an architect, but his goal was just as concrete. And she had no doubt that he would succeed in creating the biggest media empire in the world. With both a ruthless singularity of purpose and a relentless ambition that relegated everything outside of work to the outer edges of his life, how could he fail?

Not that she cared any more.

After this weekend, Omar's obsession would no longer have anything to do with her. What mattered now was getting through the next twenty-four hours.

So don't make everything about your soon-to-be ex-husband, she told herself. *Keep things polite and impersonal. Most important of all, stay away from the past.*

She cleared her throat. 'It's difficult to believe this was all desert.'

'The desert is still here.' His eyes flickered past her to the window. 'Outside the city it stretches for hundreds of thousands of miles. Up until two hundred years ago all of this…' he gestured to the gleaming skyscrapers '…

was covered with sand. The tribes that moved into the region stuck to the coast. They fished and traded with their neighbours, and then they started diving for pearls.'

She was interested despite herself. 'Pearls?'

He nodded. 'Saltwater pearls. But they found something even more valuable. They found gold.'

She felt the limo starting to slow. Seconds later, it stopped, but before she had a chance to process the moment of arrival the car door had opened, and she was stepping out into the hot night air.

'This way.'

Omar was beside her now and, flanked by the two blank-faced bodyguards she had seen at the airport, they made their way to a discreet entrance with a uniformed doorman. Then there was more blissful cool as she followed Omar through a stunning marble foyer into a lift.

The doors closed and her pulse dipped as she suddenly realised that the bodyguards had melted away. For the first time since he had walked into the hospital in Idaho, they were alone. And even though she couldn't see his eyes, she knew that Omar had registered it too.

She felt a flicker of heat, low in her belly. They were standing so close it would take no effort to lean into the space between them and press her mouth against his. To pull his hard, muscle-bound body against hers and feel his heat radiate through the thin cotton of her dress.

From the corner of her eye she saw him turn towards her and her pulse accelerated. Her face felt as if it was on fire. She needed to step away, but she didn't dare move.

Polite and impersonal, she reminded herself quickly and, staring straight ahead, said, 'I didn't know they'd found gold here.'

Did he sense the tension behind her remark? Could he hear the pounding of her heart, the hum of her blood? It was impossible to say. Knowing Omar…probably. It was not a comforting thought.

'I was talking about black gold. Oil. People here got very rich, very quickly, and now it's a city of superlatives.' He reached up and pressed his palm against a screen. Instantly the lift started to move. 'The biggest, the tallest, the fastest—'

No wonder, then, that he called it home, she thought.

The powerful muscles of his arm were capturing her gaze and holding it as her heartbeat tripped over itself. Omar was the flesh-and-blood embodiment of all superlatives. Darkest eyes. Softest mouth. Most passionate lover…

She could still remember that first time they'd kissed at her father's ranch. How much she'd wanted it. How much she'd feared it. Could remember the slowing of her pulse and how his lips had moved over hers, deliberately, thoroughly, and how she had melted into him, her head spinning, her breath fluttering in her throat.

It was dangerous, the effect he had on her. When he was close her brain seemed to short-circuit, Her sense of self-preservation got swamped by his beauty, his assurance, his unfiltered masculinity.

And nothing had changed, she thought, remembering their last kiss—the one that had happened twenty-four hours ago in a field in Idaho.

Her belly clenched and, feeling his eyes on her face, she jerked her gaze away, hating herself, despising the effect even the memory of his mouth had on her body. Hating, too, how, lost in the heat of desire, she had forgotten the most important superlative of all.

The biggest betrayal.

And its aftermath.

All those hours on her own, curled up on the floor of the bathroom, losing the baby she had only just learned was growing inside her.

Her hand moved jerkily to touch her stomach.

She still didn't know what had prompted her to take a pregnancy test. Had she not done so, she would probably have thought it was just a late period that was heavier than usual. In some ways, she wished she hadn't ever known. But then she would never have had those few precious days of shock and wonder and hope. Or the chance to say goodbye.

Her breath felt thin and light. Afterwards, she wished she had told Omar about the pregnancy, but it had been too late by then. Too complicated. Too devastating. Too irrelevant. Anything she'd planned to say had been swallowed up by her anger and hurt.

Besides, it had all been over—so what would have been the point of saying anything? And she hadn't wanted the footnote to their marriage to be just another meaningless apology.

She felt a twinge of guilt. Maybe she should have told him… But there was no point thinking about that now. This time tomorrow he would be out of her life for good. Better to concentrate her energies on surviving the ordeal ahead.

The lift stopped and the doors opened onto another beautiful marble interior. Lined up waiting for them were four women, all wearing neat black uniforms, and a tall man in a dark suit.

'As-salam alaykum.' Stepping forward, the man inclined his head.

'Wa'alaykum as-salam.' Delphi smiled stiffly, glancing round the beautiful empty foyer.

'Samir, this is my wife, Sayeda Delphi.' Omar turned towards her. 'Samir is in charge of the household staff.'

'Welcome home, sir…madam. I hope you had a restful flight.'

Delphi froze. *Home!* The word punched a hole in her composure. What did he mean by that? Had she misheard him or was it some kind of language mix-up?

Something of what she was feeling must have shown in her face, because in the next moment Omar had fired off a round of Arabic, and Samir had inclined his head again, then turned and retreated, accompanied by the women.

'What's going on?' She turned to Omar, her eyes narrowing. 'You said I was staying at a hotel.'

He strode past her without answering, the movement of his body illuminating his path just as if he was some mythical god. For a moment she hesitated, but where was she going to go? She swore softly and then, gritting her teeth, she followed him inside, panic swelling against her breastbone as an expanse of pale walls and richly coloured furnishings in Pharaoh hues of blue, yellow, white and black led into a huge open-plan living area.

Omar stopped and turned to face her.

'No, I said you would be staying at the Lulua, and you are.'

She stared at him, hating him, fighting the desire just to look at him in wonder. Despite the long flight, and the heat and the tension between them, he looked cool and relaxed. Now she was fighting a different desire: to take off her espadrilles and throw them at his head.

'There are two parts to the complex. The hotel next door.' His eyes locked with hers. 'And the private apartments.'

Private. The word shivered across her skin, and she stared at him mutely. Warning bells were ringing so loudly in her head that she was surprised the fire service hadn't turned up.

'And where will you be staying?' she asked slowly.

He smiled then. It was a smile that might spread across the face of the villain in a film. The sort of smile that denoted mockery or madness, and usually pre-empted a nasty surprise for the heroine or hero. So even before he replied she knew what his answer would be.

'Why, here, of course.'

Tipping back his head, he stretched out his

shoulders, just as if he was still her husband, returning home after a long working day. Only that had never happened, she thought savagely, because after the first week of married life she had given up waiting for him and gone to bed alone.

'There's no "of course" about it,' she said.

Her voice sounded breathless and high, but for once she didn't care that she was revealing her feelings. 'Private' plus Omar equalled a bad idea, she thought, her skin shrivelling with panic and with something else—something she wasn't even going to acknowledge, much less give a name to.

She watched his forehead crease.

'Why are you making this into such a big deal? It's a triplex apartment. Our paths will hardly cross. It's quiet and private. There's a gym, a sauna and a pool. There's even a cinema room.'

'I don't care about the facilities,' she snapped. 'This isn't what I agreed to.'

She had thought she would be staying at a hotel. Hotels were neutral spaces populated by strangers. Any space she shared alone with Omar was never going to be neutral.

His dark eyes hadn't moved from her face. 'What you agreed to, Delphi, is that while you're here in Dubai there is no "I". There's only "we". And *we* will be staying in *our* apartment—together.'

She stared at him mutinously. 'I'd rather stay at the hotel.' She didn't want to share this apartment with him and be reminded of the apartment she had lived in when she had believed herself loved. The apartment she had left behind. She needed time alone to steel herself for the ordeal to come.

'The hotel is fully booked.'

'Then I'll stay at another hotel.'

A muscle flickered along his jawline. 'That's not possible.'

Her eyes found his. 'Don't be ridiculous, Omar. They can't all be fully booked.'

'I wouldn't imagine so, no.' His tone was cool and hard. 'But it's not appropriate.'

She stared at him, trying to breathe normally, stunned by his response. 'For a woman to stay in a hotel on her own?' The intensity of his focus was making her skin prickle.

'In this situation, you're not just a woman. You're my wife, and the daughter-in-law of Rashid Al Majid—so, *yes*, it would be inappropriate for you to stay at a hotel on your own. Besides, why would you want to when we have a perfectly good apartment of our own?'

Did he have no understanding of what it was doing to her, being here with him? And what was it going to be like, having to pretend to his entire family that they were still in love?

She looked up at him, disbelief vying with fury. 'You really want me to answer that?'

'Obviously,' he said, breaking the taut silence. 'That's what husbands and wives do. They have conversations. Discussions. But, as we both know, I'd have better luck squeezing blood from a stone than getting you to answer a question about yourself.'

Her eyes widened. 'That's not true. Or fair.'

'Fair?'

His voice scraped against her skin like the heat-charged air.

'You walked out on our marriage. No note. No forwarding address. Tell me, how does that equate to being *fair*?'

The injustice of his words almost knocked her off her feet. It hadn't been about fairness… just survival. And she wanted to throw the truth in his face. But where would hurling accusations at him take her? She felt her stomach lurch. She knew where. It would take her back to a place she never wanted to revisit. Back to the past…back to her parents' last row.

She took a deep breath, bit back the comment she wanted to make, and made herself speak calmly. 'I didn't come here to talk about our marriage, Omar. I came here to go to your father's birthday party.'

'You mean the party you forgot about?'

She hated him then. Hated how he twisted everything. In Omar's world he was never wrong. *She* was wrong for not opening up more to him. *She* was to blame for not simply accepting that his work took priority over everything else in his life. For not accepting his apologies and forgiving him. And now she was at fault for not remembering his father's party.

Her heart was beating out of time. 'At least I only forgot a party. You forgot you had a wife.'

'Not this again.'

Her pupils flared. 'Yes, this again.'

He stared at her for a long moment, and she sensed that he was battling to control his temper.

'If you're talking about my working hours, you knew who I was when you married me. I don't just have some little nine to five office job. I run a global business. I'm responsible for thousands of people. So, *yes*, I work late, and I travel often. And if you're talking about London, I didn't forget you, Delphi. *You* changed the plan. *Twice*. And I understood why that happened—why you needed the time and space to get things straight in your head. But you didn't extend to me the same courtesy. You refused to understand why I couldn't just ditch my plans. You didn't even try. You just did what you always do: deflected everything I said and threw up more barriers between us.'

She could feel his frustration, his bafflement that he hadn't been able to stop that from happening. But it wasn't the same, she thought, replaying the twisting, conflicted process of her thoughts at that time. She had been confused and scared about going back to England. It was her birthplace, but it was also the scene of so much pain and loss. And then she had found out she was pregnant, and that had added in an extra layer of complication, a sudden and unexpected hope, clear and bright like a flame.

Only the last thing she needed right now was to think about that. She was suddenly furious with herself for picking at a scar that needed to be left well alone.

'There was nothing to understand,' she said flatly. 'It was just another business meeting.'

He shook his head. 'It was a once-in-a-lifetime business meeting. If I hadn't had that conversation with Bob Maclean, he would have had it with someone else. And I would have missed my chance.'

Her hands curled into fists, her nails scoring the palms. He was impossible. Impossibly stubborn and self-righteous and blinkered. How could she have let him kiss her again? Worse, how could she have liked it so much?

She took a breath. 'Which would have been annoying, but I'm sure you would have got over it.'

His dark gaze tore into her. 'It wasn't just about me. I was doing it for us. For our future.'

Something in his words made her stomach curl in on itself. 'We don't have a future. We just have a brief, unhappy past and a truly dysfunctional present.'

'Because you expected marriage to be one long honeymoon.'

Surprise, surprise—that was her fault too.

'Not based on personal experience. How long did we get in Maui? Two days?'

'Three,' he said curtly. 'And I apologised for that at the time. Just like I apologised for not coming to London with you. I don't know what else I could have done.'

And that was the problem, Delphi thought, staring at Omar's handsome, arrogant face. With his tailored suits and Harvard business degree he thought he was such a modern male. But his attitude to relationships might have come straight out of a nineteen-fifties soap opera. For him, an apology was the beginning and the end of his input. That was his part over and done with. Her job was to accept the apology and move on. If she didn't, then *she* was the problem.

A heaviness was creeping over her. Like the flu…only not the flu. It was more a sense of sadness and defeat, like before. She felt empty, fragile. *Lonely.*

But that was one of the consequences of thinking you could trust someone with your happiness. Because you loved them, and you thought they loved you, you gave them power, expecting and believing and hoping they would use it to protect you and cherish you and heal you.

Instead, they hurt you.

And she knew that.

She'd known it when her parents died, and her aunts had fought over her like hyenas with a bone…only the bone had been her trust fund. Later, girls at school and their mothers had seemed so caring and concerned for her—until she'd read about herself online, with quotes from the same 'concerned' but anonymous family friends.

It was why she'd held herself apart for so long. Why she worked with horses and not humans. But then she had met Omar and it had been impossible to keep her distance. She had allowed herself to trust him, to need him…

But never again.

She felt that same flatness she had felt after returning from London. Not tiredness, exactly, just a desire to curl up and hide beneath a duvet. There was no point in any of this. He would never understand what he had done. What he had destroyed.

'Fine. You win,' she said quickly. 'I'll stay here with you.'

His face relaxed a little. But she could already sense him regrouping, planning his strategy for the next battle.

'Good. Because it might have escaped your attention, but you are being treated with all the respect and consideration afforded to my wife. Which, by the way, is more than you deserve. So perhaps for the remainder of your stay you could try not to make a drama out of every little thing that doesn't quite meet with your approval.'

She could barely swallow. Heart hammering, she stared at him. 'Are you being serious?'

'I could ask you the same question.' His expression was hard and uncompromising. 'You know, up until six weeks ago we were sharing more than a living space…we were sharing a bed. Or have you forgotten about that too?'

No, she hadn't.

His words, and more specifically the memories they evoked, rippled through the taut air and through her. Her body felt suddenly tight and yet loose, hot and cold at the same time, as she tried not to remember Omar's mouth devouring hers, and the tangle of their limbs as they fought to get past not just clothes but skin and flesh. Tried too to forget how often they had failed to undress or lie down or even make it to the bed.

Shaking inside, she blanked her mind, and looked him straight in the eye. 'Well, I'm not going to be sharing a bed with you tonight. Or any other night for that matter.'

There was a long, quivering silence, and the already strained tension in the foyer cranked up several notches.

'Oh, believe me, that won't be a problem.'

He spoke calmly, but she could sense the anger fizzing beneath his smooth, tanned skin.

'Do you honestly think I want you in my bed, in my life, after the way you've acted? I didn't come and find you in that hospital or follow you to that seedy little bar to rekindle our relationship, Delphi. I don't want to fix what you smashed into pieces. In case I didn't make it clear enough before, you're here now for one reason and one reason only. For my father, my family.' His lip curled slowly and deliberately, like a dog confronted by a stranger. 'And when this is over, we're done.'

Floored by the hostility in his voice, she took a step back. It hurt more than it should. More than she wanted it to. But she would never let it show. She was done with sharing secrets with this man.

'Finally, we agree on something.' Her heart was aching so much that she felt as if she was about to double over. 'Now, if there's nothing more, I suggest you tell me where my room is.'

CHAPTER FOUR

SHE WAS IMPOSSIBLE. *Utterly impossible.*

Walking into his bedroom—the master bedroom, the bedroom he should be sharing with his wife—Omar let loose a torrent of expletives. With an effort of superhuman willpower, he just managed to resist the temptation to slam the door. Although, frankly, he'd had more than enough provocation to tear down the apartment with his bare hands. In fact, he was feeling so thwarted, so infuriated with Delphi, he could probably raze the entire city back to the sand it had come from.

He took a breath, tried to steady his heart rate.

Outside a moon hung in the darkening sky and drawn perhaps by its uncomplicated serenity, he snatched up the remote control by his bed and watched it, his mouth taut, his shoulders straining against his T-shirt as the door to the balcony slid open silently.

Taking a deep, calming breath, he stalked into the darkness. The air was still hot, much hotter than the apartment, but he didn't care. He needed distance from Delphi.

He had bought this apartment off-plan nearly three years ago and stayed here maybe seven or eight times. He had never once taken time to stand and stare at the view. Now, though, he was grateful for it. The endless merging darkness of the sea and sky was serene, tranquil, calming, and with Delphi throwing obstacles in the way of each and every suggestion he made he was going to need all the help he could get to stay calm.

His mouth twisted. *Easier to say than do.*

Six weeks ago, when he'd returned home from work to find Delphi gone, he had been blinded, speechless, numb with shock, and then furious that she had given up on their marriage. Stealing away as if he was some one-night stand instead of the husband she had promised to love until death parted them.

His shoulders were suddenly rigid with tension.

Her leaving had done more than break his heart. The shock of walking into the empty, echoing apartment had raised memories he'd worked hard to forget. Literally. Until he'd met Delphi, his homes had simply been assets, accruing value. All his energies, all his time, had been spent working. He'd lost count of how many all-nighters he'd pulled. But what did a little physical exhaustion matter if it helped achieve his goal of having something of his own that would finally catch the eye of his father?

And if Delphi had been the wife she'd promised to be then his dreams would have been her dreams too. But instead of supporting him unconditionally she had acted like a sulky child. Retreating into silence whenever he had to work late or take a phone call over supper.

In the days and nights that had followed her leaving, his hurt pride had stoked his anger and he'd feverishly and repeatedly imagined the moment when he finally caught up with her and could angrily demand an explanation.

But then he'd remembered his father's party and ensuring that Delphi was by his side had become his new priority. He knew he could track her down. All he'd needed was time or luck.

He'd got lucky.

Hanging up on the cowboy who'd called to tell him Delphi was in hospital, he'd promised himself that he would stay cool and detached. Unfortunately that resolution had been broken the moment he'd stepped between those curtains. Delphi had looked up at him and he'd seen the same old wariness and intransigence in her brown eyes.

But her stubbornness had simply made him determined to win.

And he had won.

She was here in Dubai.

Only now it was starting to feel less like a victory and more like an act of unparalleled foolishness on his part to have brought her here. His mouth twisted. The same foolishness that had driven him to arrogantly pursue her when even her own family had warned him of the challenge of doing so.

'I like you, Omar,' her adoptive father, Dan, had said to him. 'You're smart, and hard-working, and I'm guessing you don't usually have too much trouble attracting women.'

No, he didn't. Of course he hadn't gone so far as to actually agree out loud with Dan, but nor had he denied it. Why would he? Ever since he was a teenager women had thrown themselves at him.

Until Delphi.

'I'm not interested in other women, Dan,' he'd said, with the complacent arrogance of a man who took it for granted that he could win any woman he wanted. 'I'm interested in your daughter.'

'And I know my daughter.' Dan had smiled

wryly. 'She doesn't trust easily. You won't get reins on her unless she feels safe.'

An understatement, he thought, his fingers curling around the rail, tightening against the still-warm metal. Delphi was ice-cool and aloof with outsiders. An expert at keeping people at arm's length and her emotions in check. Never before in his life had he worked so hard, committed so much time and energy and effort into trying to understand anyone.

It had taken three months to break through the barriers she had built against the world, and when finally she had stopped running, stopped deflecting, and opened up a little to him, it had been easy to see why she found it so hard to trust. Her parents' lives and deaths had marked her out as a target for all kinds of unscrupulous people. If Dan hadn't stepped in, who knew what would have happened to her?

Only the trouble was nobody was more aware of that fact than Delphi. It was why she was so hard to pin down. Why persuading her to trust him had been a Herculean task.

But he had done it.

Watching her with her horses, he'd seen how she let them make choices, let them set the pace. He'd seen her patience as she'd waited for them to come to her. And he had done the same. He had watched, waited, held his breath…

Sliding that ring on to her finger in Vegas, he'd thought—hoped—he'd done enough.

Some hope.

She'd been so insecure, so certain that he would let her down. It had been almost as if she was waiting for it to happen…looking for it to happen. Maybe that was what their marriage had been about? Not love. Not him. But proving herself right.

Why else would she refuse to give him—give *them*—a second chance? She had deemed him deficient, unnecessary, and cut him out of her life with the ruthless, dispassionate precision of a surgeon removing a ruptured appendix.

His fingers twitched against the warm metal.

Not completely dispassionate, he thought, remembering how she had softened against him back in Idaho.

In the weeks after she'd left, he had imagined a life without her. He had told himself that she was a burden, an impossible weight to carry. But in those few shimmering, electric moments, he had forgotten all that. Suddenly there had been no barriers between them, physical or otherwise. Her body had fitted against him seamlessly, as it had so many times before, and he would have held her close like that until the end of time if those actual real-life fireworks hadn't broken the spell.

He ran his hand over his face, wishing he could as easily erase the memory of Delphi's mouth on his.

But it was going to stay a memory, he told himself grimly. Once upon a time he might have believed he was strong and sane enough for both of them—not anymore. He was done with trying to make sense of what went on inside that beautiful head of hers.

Bracing himself against the ache in his groin, he stared up at the moon. Here in Dubai, and in most of the Arab world, the moon was an important symbol. There were lots of documented reasons for that. His favourite was the story his mother had used to tell him when he was a child, of how, to avoid the heat of the day, his ancestors had used to travel by night along the desert trade routes, and therefore their navigation had been dependent upon the position of the moon and stars.

If only the moon could guide him through the next twenty-four hours... Truthfully, it couldn't make a bigger mess of things than he and Delphi had, he thought sourly, yanking off his T-shirt as he walked back into the bedroom.

Staring out of the window at the blue-black sky, Delphi felt her stomach tighten. Although she wasn't quite sure why, given that this was the third time in as many days that she had found herself sitting reluctantly in the back of an oversized car with her estranged husband. This time, they were en route to her father-in-law's residence in the exclusive Emirates Hills suburb of the city.

Then again, she *was* just about to meet Omar's entire family for the first time.

And the last.

And if that wasn't enough of a reason to make the butterflies in her stomach go into a tailspin, Omar was wearing a black *kandura*—the traditional robe worn by men throughout the Gulf States.

She glanced over to where he was sitting, his long legs stretched out casually, his dark-eyed profile fixed on the phone in his hand. Her pulse twitched. He looked good in a suit; in a *kandura* he looked sublime. There was something about the austere collarless robe which emphasised the raw, uncompromising masculine beauty of the man wearing it.

Her eyes snagged on the phone in his hand. Pity about his choice of accessory. Of course you could take the man out of the boardroom, but you couldn't stop him doing business. Not if that man was Omar Al Majid, anyway.

As if sensing her focus, Omar looked up and across the car. Suddenly finding herself the object of his hard, steady gaze, she felt her skin begin to sting. She swallowed, her mouth dry and tight. Only he had this way of skewering her with his eyes—but how? And why did he still have the power to reach inside her and make her body hum with nervous energy?

It was a strangely intimate moment in a day during which he had barely spoken to her. Waking mid-morning, she had showered and dressed, but it had been Samir who greeted her. And Samir who had shown her around the apartment, which was as large and well-appointed as Omar had told her it was.

Of Omar there had been no sign. Her mouth thinned. Actually, that wasn't quite true. There had been the usual familiar laptop left open on a table with a bowl of dates and a cup of strong, black coffee cooling beside it, but the man himself was, according to Samir, tied up on important calls.

No change there, then. Not that it was any of her business any more. She was just here to show her face at the party.

Suddenly she was trembling inside, and in an effort to calm herself she smoothed out an imaginary crease in her skirt.

Maha, the stylist Omar had provided, had chosen it for her. She had arrived after lunch, with rails full of beautiful dresses in every colour imaginable, and Delphi was intensely grateful that it hadn't been left to her to choose. Dressing up was not her thing. Day to day, she lived in jeans, T-shirts, and boots. She'd had to borrow a dress and those unbelievably painful sandals from Ashley to go to the barbecue. Even on her wedding day she had kept it low-key, choosing to wear a cream cashmere sweater with a pair of matching tailored shorts.

She glanced down, her heart bumping against her ribs. This dress, though, was anything but low-key.

Made of sunset-gold iridescent sequins, it was a one-of-a-kind couture piece—two pieces, actually. A bandeau top with a tulle overlay and fitted sleeves, and a shamelessly over-the-top full skirt.

'Don't you think it's a bit much?' she had asked Maha.

Maha had shaken her head vigorously, her glossy ponytail flicking from side to side like a cheerleader's hair at a football match. 'Just because we have a modest dress code it doesn't mean you need to be invisible.' She smiled. 'I know you're worried because it's your father-in-law's birthday party, and he is a very important man. But people here are proud about who they are and what they've achieved. Trust me—if all eyes are on you, that is a good thing.'

In other words, go big or go home.

'Going big' was not something that came naturally to her. When she was a child, Ianthe and Dylan had used her as an accessory, taking her to movie premieres and concerts and once, famously—and to the disapproval of parents all over the world—to a nightclub.

As far as she was concerned, all eyes being on her was very bad. She hated the flashing cameras, the strangers calling out her name and telling her to smile. At least she wouldn't have to worry about that at the party. The Al Majid name didn't just open doors: it closed them. There would be no press or curious members of the public craning their necks to see what the orphaned daughter of Ianthe Reynolds and Dylan Wright looked like now.

Just one unfeeling, infuriatingly arrogant husband, she thought, glancing over at Omar.

'Something to say, Delphi?' he said softly.

Plenty, she thought, but it would be wasted on him. After all, in less than twenty-four hours he would be out of her life for good.

Keeping that fact at the front of her mind, she shrugged. 'I was just thinking it's a shame you didn't leave your phone at home. But then I suppose that would mean you'd be off-grid, and you've never let anything, including our marriage, get in the way of work before. Why should your father's ninetieth birthday be any different?'

A cool shiver ran down her spine as he gave her a long, steady look. 'I was replying to a message from my sister Jalila. She texted me to say how much she is looking forward to finally meeting you.'

She felt her body tense. There was an edge to his voice—probably because she'd called him out for always being on his phone—but it felt like an attack. As if it was her fault that she and Jalila had never met. But Omar had never encouraged her to meet his family.

She had met his parents briefly in New York, a month after their wedding. What she'd noticed most about his mother, Maryam, was how much younger she was than her husband. And as for Rashid… Like his son, he was a master at controlling social situations, so it was hard to say for sure, but she'd got the impression that Rashid was either bored or distracted, maybe both. Either way, they hadn't stayed long.

And, despite his having sixteen of them, she had never met any of his half-siblings. For some reason she still didn't understand it had just never happened. But then she was so close to her own family she hadn't given it much thought.

She felt a sharp pang of homesickness, like

she had in the hospital. Her brothers Ed, Scott and Will had welcomed Omar into their homes and into their hearts, and they had encouraged her to let down her guard, to stop shielding herself from her feelings.

Her heart thudded. Thinking about telling them that her marriage was over made her feel sick. It was even worse when she thought about Dan. Even though he had done nothing but love and support her, she knew he would blame himself and that she was going to break his heart.

Just as her mother, Ianthe, had done.

'I need you to do something.'

Omar's voice cut across her thoughts and she stared at him warily. 'You've dragged me halfway around the globe to spare your blushes, so I think I'm already doing enough, don't you?'

Immediately she wished she hadn't said anything. His expression was like stone, but there was a glitter in his dark eyes that made her breath catch.

'Out of the two of us, Delphi, I'm not the one prone to blushing.'

He paused and she saw something in his eyes that darted though her, hot and unchecked like the lick of a flame.

'But perhaps you need me to refresh your memory.'

For a moment she couldn't breathe, couldn't

think of any kind of comeback. She was swamped by the slow, heavy pounding of her heart. It was true. Omar knew exactly how to make her skin grow warm, in public and in private, with his eyes, his hands, his tongue…

She swallowed. 'I don't require any reminders. That's why I want a divorce.'

He stared at her steadily. 'And, as I told you before, until that happens, you're still my wife. So tonight, for reasons I shouldn't have to explain, you will need to wear a ring.'

There was a short, stiff silence, and then he held out his hand. Heart hammering, she stared down at the fine silver band. It looked so similar to the one Omar had given her in Vegas she might have thought it was that very ring. Only she knew the original was tucked into the pocket of her toiletries bag.

Don't, she warned herself.

But it was too late, she was already there in the Little Chapel of Love, with Omar beside her, tall and handsome and serious, his dark eyes holding her steady, holding her safe.

And yet she hadn't believed it was happening, that she was really there, exchanging vows with this shockingly beautiful man. She'd had to keep touching him, her hand trembling against his chest and his arm, even after he'd slid the ring on her finger, needing to make sure that he was real and that she wasn't dreaming.

Beneath her ribs, her heart began beating unevenly. She had been wrong. For her, happy endings could only ever be a dream; that was something she'd known since waking to find herself an orphan at the age of four. Only back in Vegas, lost in the velvet-soft focus of his gaze she hadn't wanted to believe it was true.

She did now.

Her pulse jerked as beside her, jaw tightening, Omar leaned forward. 'Here, let me.'

'No. I'll do it,' she snapped.

She wouldn't let him take the memory of that day and turn it into something ugly. It was all she had left, and it wasn't going to be ruined along with everything else.

Ignoring the tenderness in her chest, she picked up the ring and slid it onto her finger. It fitted perfectly—obviously—but that only rubbed more salt into the wound. It should be too big or too small, she thought dully.

The car was slowing and, turning towards the window again, she caught a glimpse of wide marble steps flanked by men in dark suits. And then the limousine stopped. Her heart was racing; she could taste the adrenaline in her mouth. Parties, people, crowds…they were so not her thing.

If only she could stay here in the car. Just drop Omar off and then go back to the apartment—better still the airport. But if she did that then she wouldn't get her divorce. Or at least not quickly or easily. And slow and difficult would just mean more pain for everyone.

All she had to do was get through the next few hours and it would be over. She would have kept her side of the bargain and she could get the hell out of Dodge. Or, in her case, Dubai.

'This way, darling.'

Omar was standing beside her, his hand outstretched. She blinked, the sudden casual intimacy of his words knocking the air out of her lungs, and then held out her hand and let him lead her through the gleaming white hallway.

Her first thought was how unlike her own family home it was. The ranch house was large and sprawling, but really it was five thousand square feet of dimly lit log cabin with stone fireplaces and worn leather sofas.

This was a real-life palace. With each step she took, polished metal and crystal chandeliers jostled with huge modern canvases and centuries-old artefacts to grab her attention. Clearly Maha had been right, she thought, remembering what the stylist had said to her. People here were proud about who they were and what they had achieved.

'You're very quiet.' Omar glanced over at her. 'Are you plotting your escape? Or my demise?'

She bit into her lip to stop it from curving into a smile. She had forgotten that side to him. The side that could make her smile and laugh. Unlike both her parents, smiling had never come naturally to her. But making her laugh was one of the ways Omar had broken down her barriers. It was why he was the first, the only man she had given her heart to.

Her eyes paused on his arresting face beneath the *ghutra*. Although other things had played a part too…

She swallowed and looked away. The sound of voices was filtering through the walls. And music. Soft, lilting, rhythmic. It reminded her of Vegas and Omar teaching her the *dabke*, a traditional Arabic wedding dance, in their room as the sun rose on the first day of their married life. They'd danced and laughed and ended up back in bed.

Now they were walking towards two huge bronze doors and, focusing her attention on what lay on the other side, she pushed back against the wave of nostalgia rising inside her.

'Both. But I would need two hands.'

Her words fluttered between them, foolish and unthinking, like moths bashing into glass.

'Not always,' he said slowly. 'Sometimes you managed perfectly well without the use of either.'

Their eyes locked and she stared at him, the air leaving her body. There was no point pretending that she didn't understand what he was talking about. She could see it as clearly as if she was there, feel it as if it was happening… their bodies twisting against the sheets and then his hand catching her wrists to stretch them above her head as he thrust deeper and deeper, until she was arching against him, mindless and moaning.

She shivered all the way through, hating herself, hating the fact that even now she could feel this way.

'Things change. I've changed.'

The music was getting louder. At the margins of her vision, she sensed rather than saw two men step forward, and then the doors swung open and her footsteps and her breathing faltered.

They had arrived at the party.

But she barely registered the huge, high-ceilinged room, or the guests turning to look at them. Drawing a jagged breath, she tugged her hand away, but he simply tightened his grip.

'If you're planning on making a scene, I'd advise against it,' he said quietly.

Heart pounding fiercely, she looked over at the man filling the space beside her. 'I'm perfectly in control of my emotions, thank you.'

The corner of his mouth curled, but there was no humour in his dark eyes. 'Then clearly you haven't changed at all. Perhaps if you had our marriage might have had a chance.'

She blinked as a camera flashed to her left.

'It's okay,' Omar murmured. 'It's a private photographer. My father likes to have a record of family events.'

'Omar!' A tall man with a close-cut greying beard stepped forward, his dark eyes widening with happiness. 'I heard you'd arrived, little brother.'

Omar smiled. 'Hamdan.' The two men embraced. 'It's good to see you too.'

Watching him, Delphi felt her stomach tighten. Nobody would know that she was here under duress, obligation. But she could sense Omar's tension. It was there in the rigidity of his body and the tightness in his jaw even as he smiled.

'Not as good as it is to see you. Don't leave it so long next time.' Hamdan squeezed Omar's shoulder, then turned, his face growing serious. 'And you must be Delphi.' He inclined his head. 'I am Hamdan, Omar's eldest brother. Welcome, finally, to Dubai.'

She knew all the children of his father's first wives were older than Omar, but Hamdan was much older—old enough to be his father or hers.

Hiding her surprise, Delphi smiled. 'Thank you. It's lovely to meet you.'

Over the next few hours she repeated that sentence more times than she could count, as one by one Omar's siblings came up to greet him and welcome her, only varying it once when Omar led her through the crowded room to meet his parents.

Then she said, 'It's lovely to see you again.'

As the only one of Rashid's children not living in the Middle East, she had thought that Omar might be treated like the prodigal son by his father. But although Rashid's greeting was affectionate, his blue gaze moved on with surprising speed.

Still, gazing round the room, it was impossible for her not to feel a twinge of guilt as her eyes leapfrogged Hamdan to each of Omar's siblings in turn. Marriage and family were clearly important to the Al Majids. Only now, just like her mother had done before her, she was going to blow everything apart. Shatter the bedrock of their lives by divorcing their son and brother.

Heart pumping, she glanced sideways at Omar. Was he thinking the same thing? Was that why his hand felt so rigid? Her chest squeezed tight, the pain suddenly too big for her body. It made no sense, given the current state of their relationship, but she couldn't bear to think that he was suffering.

'Excuse me, Delphi.' It was Hamdan, his handsome face apologetic. 'Would it be all right if I just borrowed Omar for a couple of moments?'

She nodded, her smile aching as Omar followed his brother through the guests, emotions she had managed to contain for weeks now clawing at her, overwhelming her. Why had she ever agreed to do this?

A flash caught her eye from the other side of the room, where the photographer was now taking pictures of Omar's father and his wives. Her hands clenched. She knew it was all perfectly legitimate, but it was making her nervous. Maybe she could find somewhere quiet to sit out the rest of the party. She turned, hoping she might slide discreetly away—

'Delphi!'

A beautiful woman in an exquisite flute-sleeved robe the colour of ripe pomegranates was standing in front of her.

'Sorry, I didn't mean to startle you. I just wanted to say hi, and that I love your dress. You look beautiful. You *are* beautiful.'

'Thank you.' Delphi smiled. She wasn't good at small talk, but somehow this woman made it easy for her to say, 'I love the colour of yours. It's an amazing party, isn't it?'

The woman nodded. 'What's amazing is that Baba agreed to cut short a business trip to be here. Oh, I'm Jalila, by the way—Omar's sister.'

So 'Baba' must be Rashid. But surely he wasn't still working? Delphi felt her stomach clench, but there was no time to pursue that thought.

'I'm the one you haven't met.' Jalila laughed. 'Although, to be fair, you might not have noticed there are so many of us.'

Delph screwed up her face. 'I have to admit I did lose count after I got to double figures.' She smiled at Jalila. All of Omar's siblings were good-looking, and they shared his dark hair and eyes, but with her flawless skin and fine bone structure Jalila was the one who most resembled him.

'It's fine, honestly.' Leaning towards her, Jalila lowered her voice. 'Just tell me, though, did Hamdan introduce everyone in age order or alphabetically?'

Delphi hesitated. 'I think it might have been age order.'

Jalila rolled her eyes. 'He does that because

otherwise Aisha and Ahmad would come before him. Brothers—honestly.'

Now Delphi laughed. 'I know what you mean. I have three, and I love them, but they can be a real pain.'

'Think yourself lucky. I have nine.' Jalila smiled then, almost shyly. 'But you got my favourite one, and I'm really glad about that.'

Delphi frowned. 'You are?'

Jalila nodded slowly. 'Honestly, none of us ever imagined Omar would tie the knot, and if he did we thought it would all be planned out, with a mile-long agenda. But it was so romantic...getting married on impulse like that. That's how I know he must be crazy about you.'

Wordless, Delphi stared at Omar's sister. Her hands were shaking, and she was fighting so many crazy and contradictory thoughts and feelings that her head was spinning. And some of those conflicting emotions must have shown on her face because the next moment Jalila took hold of Delphi's hands.

'Sorry, I didn't mean to be so forward. I know we've only just met, but I'm so happy Omar's found love. I know he's rich and gorgeous...' she screwed up her face as if the opposite were true '...but I also know how intense he can be, how fixated he is on proving himself.'

Proving himself? Delphi stared at her in confusion. Proving what? To whom? Her eyes flickered across the room to where Omar stood out from the crowd, and not just because he was taller than most of the other men in the room. His face was a wonder—all dark shadows and gold highlights—and his smile made him look as if he was posing for a photograph. Not the kind of man who needed to prove himself to anyone.

Jalila squeezed her hands. 'Sometimes he can be his own worst enemy, but I can tell you *get* him. And I see how my brother looks at you and I know there's nothing he wouldn't do for you. All you have to do is ask.'

Suddenly it was a struggle for Delphi to keep smiling.

Once upon a time Omar had said almost those exact words to her, and she had believed him. That was why she'd asked him to be there when she went to visit her parents' graves. Only he had let her down. Time and time again he had left her on her own. London had simply been one time too many.

'So, the magicians are circulating now.' Hamdan looked at the schedule on his phone. 'Then the aerial acrobats will start their show before the fireworks begin at midnight.'

Omar nodded, because that was what was expected of him. Frankly, he'd had more than enough fireworks over the last forty-eight hours to last a lifetime—but they were expected too.

Mohammad, his second-eldest brother, frowned. 'Unless Father decides he wants to retire early, in which case—'

Omar stood in silence, watching his brothers' talk. Despite the age gap, and their having different mothers, he loved his siblings, but being surrounded by his entire family always had the same effect on him. He felt swamped, unremarkable, irrelevant.

And probably that would never change. Because despite being thirty years old, and the CEO of a global media business, he was still the little brother. A postscript in a nappy. A last-minute addendum to an already over-long agenda.

And who bothered reading those?

Except him, of course.

He glanced over to where Rashid stood with his wives, his blue eyes moving restlessly around the room. It would take more than aerial acrobats and magicians to hold his father's attention.

Only his mother and Jalila had even come close to treating Omar as a person in his own right. Glancing across the room, he narrowed his gaze on his favourite sister with pinpoint accuracy and felt a flicker of irritation as he realised that he only knew where she was because she was talking to Delphi.

A second flicker followed, as he was forced to admit it wasn't a one-off and that he had known his wife's exact location in every second that had passed since Hamdan had towed him away from her side.

Not that he'd looked. On the contrary, his neck was aching with the effort of *not* looking. Now, though, he had an excuse, and he watched Delphi smile, then laugh with his sister, his shoulders alternately tensing then relaxing. Seeing her so at ease with Jalila was both baffling and oddly satisfying. But he was also jealous that his sister had so effortlessly done in minutes what it had taken him weeks to achieve.

Aware suddenly of a silence behind him, he turned to find his two eldest brothers watching him in amusement.

Mohammad nudged him in the ribs. 'Are we boring you, little brother?'

'Not at all—' he began.

'Go.' Hamdan grinned and gave him a little push. 'Go and talk to your beautiful wife. We can manage without you.'

But of course they could, he thought, as he made his way across the room. Throughout his life he had been extraneous to requirements. A small boy running after his much older siblings, crying and shouting, 'Wait for me!' Or tugging at the sleeve of his father's robe in a fruitless attempt to gain his attention.

It was why he had wanted to set up his business far away from his family. Here, as an Al Majid, he would have been given a high-ranking job for life, no questions asked. But he needed more. He needed something for himself. Something of his own. Something unique and beautiful and shimmering that would make his family, and in particular his father, sit up and take notice.

His eyes locked on his wife, and he felt hunger punch through his chest. In that dress, Delphi ticked all those boxes and more. In a room filled with beautiful, wealthy people and priceless objects she shone the brightest.

Breath catching, he let his gaze skim over the glittering iridescent fabric. But it wasn't just the sequins and tulle that made it hard for him not to look over and even harder to look away. She might not see it, and she certainly didn't exploit it, but as well as Ianthe's wild-honey-coloured eyes and Dylan's famous pout, Delphi had inherited her parents' ability to light up a room.

In a world where people fought tooth and nail for their fifteen minutes of fame, she was an enigma. The child of two celebrities and yet she shunned the spotlight. A beautiful young woman whose strength was her vulnerability.

And she was always vulnerable. Even now, dressed like a goddess, he could almost see her trembling inside. And outside, he thought, as Jalila took hold of his wife's shaking hands.

'You two seem to be getting along very well.'

'Finally!' Jalila turned, her forehead creasing into a mock frown as Omar kissed her on both cheeks. 'Don't bother coming to say hello, will you?'

'I tried. You were with Khalid.'

Her face softened. 'Have you seen him yet?' As he shook his head, she clutched at his arm and gave a squeal of excitement. 'Thank goodness! I'm just going to go and get him. So don't go anywhere. Either of you. Please,' she added, before turning to scamper away.

Beside him, he felt Delph stiffen. 'She won't be long.'

'It's fine. I don't mind waiting. I like her.'

He felt his stomach clench, and a quickening of his pulse as she gave him a small, tight smile. It reminded him of the first time they'd met, and he found himself responding just as he had then. Only why? It was over. Except it didn't feel over when she was standing this close…

'You look beautiful, by the way,' he said abruptly. 'I wanted to say so earlier. But I was angry.'

Was? He frowned. Was he not angry now?

Confused, he pushed the thought away. 'What I'm trying to say is that I know you don't like getting dressed up, so thank you.'

He felt the back of his neck tingle as her eyes found his. 'I was worried I'd be overdressed, but—'

They both glanced across the room at the guests in their jewel-coloured robes and glittering gold accessories.

'Looks like you have one less thing to worry about,' he said softly. Their eyes met again. 'Now you just have to get shot of your monumentally arrogant and selfish husband.'

She blinked. 'You weren't always arrogant and selfish.'

The air around them seemed to snap to attention. He stared at her, not moving a muscle, scared to move. 'Do you mean that?' There was a note in his voice he didn't quite recognise.

The pulse in her throat jerked against her pale skin.

'Sorry I took so long.'

He swore silently as Jalila returned. ‘Fahad was showing him off to the aunties, but he needs to go to sleep now, otherwise he’ll be up all night—only I wanted you to meet him first.’

Omar’s heart twitched as she held out the baby.

‘Khalid, this is your uncle Omar. Omar, this is your nephew.’

He settled the baby in the crook of his arm and gazed down into his huge brown eyes. ‘He’s beautiful, Lila.’ Throat tightening, he thumbed a feathery dark curl away from Khalid’s doe-skin cheek and kissed his forehead. Tiny, beautiful, and mesmerizingly perfect.

‘Yes, he is. Actually, he reminds me of you.’ Jalila bit her lip. ‘Baba thinks so too. He even got Auntie Maryam to find a photo of you at the same age.’

Batting away the twist of pleasure her words produced, Omar said quickly, ‘How old is he now?’

‘Six weeks. Talking of photos—yes, please. My son and my brother.’

It was the photographer. As the camera flashed, Omar caught a glimpse of Delphi’s face. She looked like a deer in the headlights, all huge panicky eyes and jerky pulse.

‘That’s enough.’ He dispatched the photographer with a jerk of his head.

'Oh, goodie.'

A waiter had materialised at his shoulder and Jalila leaned forward and snatched up a glass of orange juice.

'He's so hungry it makes me thirsty all the time. Would you like one, Delphi? Or you can have champagne. Honestly, nobody will mind.'

'No. No, thank you.'

Delphi's voice, or rather the brittle *keep-away-from-me* edge to it, jolted him out of his baby-fixated trance and he looked up in surprise. She'd seemed to be getting on with Jalila so well.

But his sister hadn't registered the change. 'It's no trouble, really. Let me—'

'I said no.' Delphi's voice rose and snapped like a sail in the wind. 'I don't want champagne. I don't want a drink. I just need some air.'

She stumbled backwards. Behind her, a magician made a dove appear out of a scrunched-up handkerchief with a theatrical flourish. Distracted, Omar glanced over and felt his body tense. Inside his head a thought, a possibility, was starting to take shape…hazy at first, then growing clearer.

'Delphi.' He reached for her but was hampered by the baby. And, swerving his outstretched hand, she sidestepped past him.

Jalila's dark eyes brimmed with tears. 'I'm sorry…' A flush was creeping over her cheeks.

'It's fine. She's still upset from the accident. Here, take Khalid.' Heart hammering, he handed the baby to his sister. 'It'll be okay.'

'She looked so pale.'

He'd have to take Jalila's word for it, he thought as he wove through the guests. He hadn't been looking at Delphi's face. He'd been too busy watching the way her hand had moved to curve protectively over her belly.

The corridor was empty.

He turned, caught a glimpse of gold.

'Delphi!'

Like Cinderella fleeing the ball, she gathered up her skirts and ran. But no woman wearing a floor-length dress and heels could outrun a man. Particularly not a man like him, who had a burning question that needed answering.

He caught her arm as she reached the gardens, his hand clamping around her waist, stopping her in her tracks.

'Let go of me.'

He tightened his grip. 'Not until you tell me the truth. Are you pregnant?'

She squirmed against him, but her strength was no match for his.

Capturing her chin, he tilted her face up to his. 'Tell me.'

Her eyes were as huge and dark as the baby's, her face pale with shock and pain as she jerked free.

'No. I'm not.' She sounded as if it hurt her to speak. 'But I was. I had a miscarriage.'

CHAPTER FIVE

OMAR STARED DOWN at Delphi. The confusion of anger and tension that had been driving him forward since she'd walked out of their home six weeks ago had dissolved, and in its place was—

Nothing.

No reply. No response. No reaction.

It was as if her words had hollowed him out, stolen not just the breath from his body but his understanding of the world, and in its place was the static rush of the ocean, like the sound when you held up a shell to your ear.

Only this rush was so big and so loud it was a roar, swallowing him whole.

He was in shock, obviously. That was why he couldn't swallow or speak. And why, despite the warmth of the evening, he felt as though his body was encased in ice.

Shock on top of shock—because just a few moments earlier he had assumed she was pregnant.

All the evidence had suggested that. Her sudden tension when he held Khalid. Her refusal to drink alcohol. The way she had touched her stomach.

Only he was wrong, and the opposite was true.

His gaze dropped to where Delphi stood now, in that astonishing glittering gown, her hand clutching the sequinned fabric, her lips parted as if she was having to take in extra breaths through her mouth.

She had been pregnant but had lost the baby. Not *the* baby, he corrected himself. *Their* baby—*his* baby. And now his heart was thumping violently against his ribs, so that even though the flagstones beneath him were literally made of rock, it felt as though he was standing in the epicentre of an earthquake.

'You were pregnant.'

He didn't know why but he needed to hear the words in his own voice to make it real. She nodded, her face taut, her gaze steady and unblinking, but beneath the stillness he could see she was fighting to hold something in, or back, or together.

'But you lost the baby. *Our* baby.'

From inside the house, he could hear the faint but clear clink of glasses and the hum of conversation. It all sounded so reassuringly normal—only how could anything be normal when there was this terrible, unalterable truth?

Delphi nodded again. Only this time as she did so her hand slipped away from the front of her dress.

It was such a small gesture, but there was a hopelessness and a hurt in it that wrenched at something inside him. He reached out unthinkingly and took her hand, because surely this was the moment when she would bring down her drawbridge and let him in? When finally, she would choose to share her loss and pain?

She was standing in front of him, straight-backed, body braced, and then she made a small choking sound and swayed forward, just as she had in the hospital.

He pulled her against him, his arms curving around her as her body crumpled. And then, so suddenly that he almost lost his balance, she was pushing against his chest, pushing him away.

'No!' Her chin jerked up. 'Don't touch me. Don't you touch me. I don't need your sympathy.'

He stared at her, a hot lava of primaeval emotions coursing through his veins.

She didn't need it, and more importantly nor was she offering any in return. His heart was beating slow and hard. Not only had she just tossed a grenade into his life and blown everything up, but she was also willing to let him stagger alone and maimed around an unrecognisable landscape.

He stared at her, his breath quickening, almost as shocked by the uncompromising and unexpected ferocity of her rejection as he was by the discovery that he had been, briefly at least, an expectant father.

The muscles in his shoulders locked painfully. In the past when Delphi had clammed up, he hadn't liked it, but he knew that she had trusted people before and been hurt, and that was why she found it so hard to lower her guard and let people in—even him.

But this was different.

This wasn't just about her. Her feelings, her needs, her wishes, her past. This was about him too. How could she keep something like that a secret from him?

He thought back to when she'd swayed forward, and he had caught her. For those few half-seconds, just like in the hospital, he'd forgotten his fury and his pain. He'd simply been relieved to have found his wife…to have found her. His Delphi.

His chest was tight, his lungs on fire. Only that implied she had been his to lose—and she had never been his. All of this proved it. Proved that he had never known what was going on in her head…never known her.

'I had a miscarriage.'

The words still burning in his brain, he stared at the woman standing in front of him, seeing a stranger.

'When did it happen?' he asked.

There was the briefest of silences, so that her answer almost overlapped his question. 'In London.'

He stared at her, with a terrible dropping feeling in his chest. How could that be? He had arrived at the London apartment late in the evening on the day she'd been to visit her parents' graves. Delphi had been quiet, but he had thought she was still angry with him for not cancelling his meeting and going with her. He had kissed her, apologised again for not being there, and asked her about her day. That was when she had told him about seeing the paparazzi and deciding not to go to the graves.

At no point had she told him that she had miscarried their baby.

'And you didn't think to mention it?' He held her gaze, shock curdling in his stomach. 'I didn't even know you were having a baby.'

Were. Past tense. Anger and misery rushed through him again. She had always been secretive, but surely this hadn't been only her secret to keep.

'How many weeks were you?'

'Eight. But I didn't realise. There was so much going on…'

Eight weeks. Two months. So, the baby would have been roughly the shape and size of a bean. For a second he couldn't feel himself breathing. *Little bean.* That was what Jalila had called Khalid when she was pregnant.

'So, when *did* you realise?'

'At about seven weeks.'

He felt like he was floating away from the confines of his body. 'I'm your husband, Delphi. You should have told me.'

She drew in a quick, unsteady breath. 'I was going to.'

'You were *going* to?' he repeated.

His chest was still warm from holding Khalid in his arms, and that hurt most of all. Knowing that he would never feel their baby's warmth or kiss its forehead.

He took a step back from her, no longer needing sympathy but space. If he hadn't asked if she was pregnant, would he have ever known about their lost baby's momentary tiny, fluttering existence? The only reason he did now was because he had made it impossible for her not to tell him.

What would have happened if he hadn't tracked Delphi down and forced her to come to Dubai?

The answer to that question tore at his insides.

'You expect me to believe you? Actually, you don't need to answer that.' A muscle flickered in his jaw. 'You don't care if I believe you or not, right?'

He scarcely recognised his own voice, but he didn't care. Nor did he believe her. Delphi had never told him anything willingly in her life. Everything had to be prised out of her. Why should this be any different?

Her eyes were huge and dark in the moonlight. 'Of course I care. But it's complicated.'

It's complicated.

He gritted his teeth. It was one of her stock get-out-of-jail-free responses to any difficult conversation—'difficult' being anything that trespassed into the personal. But personal meant relating only to one individual; this was about *him* too.

'No, it's simple, Delphi. You were pregnant with our baby, and you didn't tell me. And then you lost our baby, and you didn't tell me that either.'

The starkness of his words appeared to shock her—shock them both. But so much of his life had been spent trying to matter, and this was one occasion when he should automatically have done so—only she hadn't deemed him important enough to tell him anything.

She still didn't.

He watched her take a small step backwards, her eyes darting past his, planning her next escape route.

'Look, I know this is a shock…' she said.

Had it been a shock for her too? Not the miscarriage…the pregnancy?

Somewhere in another part of his brain he could picture Delphi in the bathroom of his New York apartment, staring down at a pregnancy test. He saw her confusion, her disbelief. And then what? Happiness? Relief? *Panic?*

He didn't know. And not knowing was like a hammer-blow to the head. But, seriously, what did he know? He'd had no idea she'd even been trying for a baby. Or maybe she hadn't. Delphi might have promised to love and cherish and honour him, but she had always disguised her feelings—held herself apart, held her past close.

Only now it appeared she had lied to him about the present too.

'But it needn't have been a shock.' He gritted his teeth. 'You could have told me about it when it happened.'

'Actually, I couldn't.' Her voice sharpened. 'Because you weren't there.'

Not here…not there…not old enough…not ready for the responsibility. He'd heard it, or some version of it, so many times before.

'So you decided to punish me by letting me find out now, here, in my father's home, at his birthday party?'

'You know that's not what happened.' Her face was flushed with anger. 'You know I'd never do that.'

'How? I don't know anything about you. You've kept things hidden from me our entire marriage…lied to my face. I have no idea what you're capable of.'

'Maybe if you'd been around a little more you would know,' she said shakily. 'Look, I didn't choose any of this. It was your decision to come after me and demand answers. Your decision to come to the hospital and then that bar. Your decision to blackmail me into coming to this party.'

He couldn't keep the sneer from his voice. 'And I thought you were here because you wanted to do the right thing.'

'I did. I do. I'm doing all this for Rashid…for your father.'

'You mean our lost baby's grandfather?'

There was a fraction of a pause as her eyes

widened. He waited for a reaction, but it didn't come. Instead, ducking her chin, she moved again to step past him.

'Where do you think you're going?' he asked quietly, blocking her. 'You're not leaving until we're finished talking.'

But she had already turned and was walking away. Not waiting for him, ignoring him. Literally giving him the cold shoulder.

Blinking the red haze from his eyes, he caught up with her in four strides, stepping in front of her. 'I am so done with chasing after you, Delphi.'

'Then stop doing it,' she hissed. 'Look, I did what you asked. I came to Dubai as your wife, and I came to your father's party. That's it. I'm done.

'I'm not done. We need to talk.'

'And you think this is the right time and place to do that?'

He glanced past her shoulder to where a group of guests had wandered out into the gardens and were now gazing admiringly at the fountains. It wasn't. But, knowing Delphi as he did, it was unlikely there ever would be a right time or place.

He clenched his fists as a burst of music, inappropriately loud and celebratory, filled the warm evening air. The fireworks were next on the schedule. Soon the gardens would be filled with guests.

'No, I suppose I don't. And you're right. You have done what I asked. So perhaps now is a good time to end this farce.'

There was a moment when her face relaxed. It was so brief that if he'd blinked, he would have missed it, but it was enough to make up his mind. Before she could react, his hand caught her elbow, and he began to frogmarch her along the path.

'What are you doing?'

Once again, she was trying to shake free of his grip, but he didn't release her. 'You want to leave. We're leaving,' he said shortly.

He had to get her out of here fast before the guests outnumbered the palm trees. Before he lost his temper in a way that would rival the upcoming pyrotechnic display.

'But the house is that way. Aren't we going to say goodbye to your parents?'

'You're here to avert gossip, Delphi, remember. Not create more. I'm the host's son and you are my wife. If we leave early, people will notice and talk.'

'I don't mind leaving alone,' she said quickly.

'Oh, I know. It's one of your major talents.'

'I just meant I can take the car back to the apartment.'

The static was back in his chest. 'You think you can run from this? You think you can just get on a plane and leave it all behind?'

Her eyes widened again, and there was a trace of uncertainty in her face. Suddenly he was fighting to stand still where he was. She was so close. All he had to do was take one step forward and kiss her…let his mouth, his hands, his body persuade her to close the gap between them as he had done so many times before.

'That's not what I said.'

'Good.'

Because this time she was going nowhere until he got some answers.

He glanced past her to where a sleek black helicopter sat squatly on its concrete apron on the lawn. Two members of his father's security team were standing beside it and, jerking his head in greeting, he barked out his instructions in Arabic.

Delphi turned, her face stiffening with shock, as one of the men leapt forward and yanked open the doors.

'After you.' Omar propelled her forward.

'No.' It was a flat, unequivocal negative. 'I don't want to.'

'You have to. We can't use the car.' He spoke with such certainty that he saw her flinch. 'For exactly the same reason that we're not going to go back and say goodbye to my parents. And we're not going to the apartment either,' he added. 'Because, as you so rightly pointed out, you and I need to talk.'

'I didn't say that. You did,' she protested, but he kept on speaking.

'And for that to happen we need somewhere quiet and private.'

Although in this instance for 'quiet and private' read 'isolated and secure'.

'Somewhere we can talk without interruption,' he continued.

Somewhere he could get answers to all the questions and conjecture swirling inside his head.

'Jalila is already worried that she's upset you. When she realises we've left the party I wouldn't put it past her to come to the Lulua. Besides, why does it matter either way where we go? It's just a few hours of your life.'

A pulse of anger beat over his skin as he thought back to that moment at the party when the shifting, disconnected pattern of dots inside his head had taken shape and he had uncovered a life-changing truth about himself.

'Surely you can give me that?' he said.

She stared at him, pale in the moonlight, as beautiful and as unreachable as the moon. 'I am not going to get into some random helicopter with you,' she said, sounding out each syllable as if she was talking to a child.

He held her gaze. 'You will, Delphi. One way or another. But it will be easier if you co-operate.'

'I have already co-operated.'

'Then you know how easy it is.'

She stared at him, and the hostility and despair in her eyes almost stopped him. But then he reminded himself that this woman had deceived him. She owed him the truth. And this time he was going to get it from her.

Gazing down at the tops of the palm trees as the helicopter rose up into the night sky, Delphi took a small, panicky breath. The smell of the leather upholstery reminded her so much of the tack room at the ranch that she felt almost faint.

Not that the man sitting beside her cared.

She turned to look at the dark-eyed, astonishingly handsome stranger who was also her husband. Her very angry, single-minded husband.

'Where are we going?'

He didn't turn to look at her. 'It's a place in the hills. About twenty minutes from here.'

She didn't know what to say to that. Right now, she felt as if she had said everything that could be said. Only it wasn't enough for Omar.

How could it be?

A pang of guilt pinched inside her chest. Whatever he might have accused her of, she hadn't planned on telling him about the miscarriage today, at his father's birthday party, surrounded by his family and friends. But then Jalila had brought over Khalid, and it had brought it all back, and the walls she had carefully built around herself to contain the hurt and pain had fallen away like petals on the wind.

Watching Omar hold the baby, seeing his fierce, brooding focus on Khalid's sweet face, had almost made her double over. Was that what their baby would have looked like too? The answer to that question had made it impossible for her to stand there another moment, and so she had done what she always did when things hurt and scared her.

She had run.

And, because he was Omar, he couldn't *not* follow. And, because he was Omar, by the time he'd caught up with her, he'd already known what question to ask.

The one she had decided nearly seven weeks ago never to answer.

And she knew that was unfair, and selfish and wrong, but the moment when it would have been possible had passed nearly seven weeks ago, in that gleaming anonymous bathroom in

London. Then she had wanted him so badly it had hurt almost as much as the cramps.

Afterwards, she had thought she had no words for what had happened. No words to express the aching sense of loss and despair, the bruising emptiness.

Her throat tightened.

But in the end, all it had taken was four. *'I had a miscarriage.'*

It was the first time she had said it out loud, and it had been a shock saying it, hearing it. Maybe that was why she was still reeling inside. That and watching Omar's face lose colour and stiffen with shock and pain.

She could still see his expression now; he had looked shattered.

Closing her eyes, Delphi leaned back in her seat. She didn't want to think about Omar's pain. It was more than she could manage when she still hadn't come to terms with her own.

For weeks now the terrible dark memory of that day had been there, keening and scrabbling at the back of her mind to be let in. But she had kept it at bay—taking on extra work at the stables, watching reruns of familiar shows on TV late into the night so she was in a near-permanent state of physical exhaustion.

Now, though, the frantic, terrifying thing

was loose, and she felt her legs start to shake just as they had in London.

It had started off as a stomachache. She'd put it down to too much adrenaline. And, arriving at the graveyard, she had felt the ache fade, swept away by a prickling rush of excitement that finally she had made it.

Over the years she had seen pictures of her parents' graves in magazines and on the internet. Their headstones weren't the first to be covered with lipstick kisses—Oscar Wilde and Marilyn Monroe were just two of the celebrities whose graves had received the same treatment. But none were as smothered in kisses as those of her parents'.

Their fans still loved them almost as much as she did, and she had waited so long to make this pilgrimage. But her excitement had been short-lived. Walking into the cemetery, she had expected to see perhaps a few particularly devoted followers. What she hadn't anticipated was spotting a pack of paparazzi lounging beneath a huge yew tree, their cameras dangling over their shoulders like avant-garde handbags…

Behind her eyelids she caught a flicker of light, and then, opening her eyes, she flinched as a volley of flashes momentarily blinded her.

Fireworks.

Heart pounding, she watched them bloom in the darkness.

Was it a cosmic joke or just coincidence that as her world was imploding, the wider world kept sending up fireworks?

If Omar noticed the fireworks he gave no indication. He sat relaxed in the pilot's seat, but his dark eyes were moving endlessly over the dials and buttons on the panel in front of him as he made minute recalibrations of height and speed.

There would be no talking now, she knew.

It was one of the things that had first attracted her to him. How he was one hundred percent in the moment. Whatever he was doing—be it driving, riding a horse, flying a helicopter—he had an incredible, unparalleled intensity of focus.

Her heartbeat slowed to a crawl. Once upon a time he had given *her* that same intensity of focus. Only then they'd got married and it had been as if he'd done enough. As if by giving her a ring and his name he thought he had proved himself once and for all. And then that focus, that glorious feeling of sunlight heating her skin, had stopped.

Her breathing sounded as if she'd been running.

Except in bed.

Then he had never faltered. And nor had she. It had been the one place she hadn't questioned herself. How could she have when together they'd been so perfect? Like dancers moving instinctively, each had known exactly, intuitively, what the other wanted, what the other needed, demanded, craved. A flickering tongue. A whisper-soft caress. Hard, urgent kisses.

It had been heat and light, havoc and passion, sensation, and sensual overload. But in the end, it hadn't been enough. *Obviously.* Marriages couldn't survive on sex alone.

'We're here.'

Omar's voice was soft, but she still jumped about a mile. Glancing out of the cockpit, she felt the hairs on the nape of her neck rise slowly.

Where was 'here'?

Panic exploding inside her like popcorn, she squinted through the glass. When Omar had told her they were going to a place in the hills, she had assumed he was talking about another of the exclusive suburbs that edged the glittering high-rise city centre, but there was nothing suburban about the view through her window.

There were lights, and the moon was huge and dazzlingly white, so it wasn't dark. But aside from the castellated outline of a pale stone building there was nothing to see but a seemingly never-ending range of stark, jagged peaks.

'You said we were going to a place in the hills,' she said slowly.

'I may have misled you.' There was a faint glitter of moonlight in his eyes. 'But I didn't think it would be a big deal. It's not as if the truth matters to you.'

A tiny shiver rippled through the helicopter. They had landed. Beside her, Omar flicked a switch and silence filled the cabin. Then he was out of his seat and, almost before she had undone her belt, opening her door and half pulling, half lifting her out of the cockpit.

'I can manage.' She pushed his hand away, watching his face harden as her stiletto heels slipped sideways on the smooth flagstones.

'Of course you can. Perish the thought that you might actually need me for anything.'

She *had* needed him. He had made it his mission for her to need and trust him. But she wouldn't make the same mistake twice.

Biting back the comment she wanted to make, she adjusted her feet. Regaining her balance, she let her eyes skate past him. They were standing in a vast courtyard surrounded by high walls. 'Who owns this place?'

'I do. It used to be a fortress.' He left a pause. 'But for now, it's going to be your home.'

She shook her head. 'My home is in Idaho.'

His face stayed blank, but his eyes narrowed just a fraction. 'If you say so. But we didn't talk in Idaho any more than we talked in New York. Perhaps we'll have more luck here.'

Without waiting for her to reply, he turned, and she watched him walk away, her heart suddenly going at ninety miles an hour. And then she hurried after him, almost tripping in her haste to keep up with him as he strode through a doorway.

'This is insane, Omar. This is not how people behave.'

Couldn't he see that rehashing the past wasn't going to change anything? It would just scrape against a wound that was barely healed.

They were walking upstairs now, and she had to pick up her skirts to keep up with him.

'Firstly, I'm not "people". I'm your husband. And talking to your partner is not generally considered a sign of insanity.'

She followed him into a room, and he stopped so abruptly she almost cannoned into him as he spun round, fatigue and frustration etched into his handsome features.

'Maybe if you accepted that…maybe if you hadn't turned every conversation into a masterclass of deflection and dissimulation…

I wouldn't have found out by chance what I should have been told by right.'

She stared at him. His words froze in the air between them like bullets in those Gun Fu films her brothers loved so much.

'And that's what this is really about, isn't it? Not me. Not our marriage. Not the truth. This is about you not being in control, not having the last word. So, actually, it's all about you.'

The look of fury in his eyes almost slammed her against the wall.

'No, that's one thing our marriage has *never* been about, Delphi. You have only ever let me into your life grudgingly.'

The word felt like a serrated blade, scraping against her skin.

'And you bumped me down your agenda for work.'

'Don't blame my work for your deceit.'

Something inside her snapped. '*You* deceived *me*. You made me think that we were a team… a partnership. Before you, I managed my life on my own and I was fine with that. I didn't want or need anyone. But you kept on pushing me to trust you, to talk to you. You made me need you. And then you were never there. You told me that I only ever had to ask for help, but when I did you let me down.'

'And I'm sorry for that.'

'You have every possible apology at your fingertips. The conditional, the phantom, the déjà vu, the *get-off-my-back*. All equally meaningless.'

'Oh, but running away when things get hard is straight out of the marriage playbook?'

Hard. The word punched the breath out of her lungs. 'This is getting us nowhere.'

'Because you're giving up.'

'And you won't—or can't let me. Because you've obsessed with winning. And if something or someone—*like me*—challenges you, then it just cements that desire to win.' Her voice was rising, and she let it. 'That's why you married me and why you came to the hospital. That's why you've dragged me out here, to the middle of nowhere. But you've wasted your time and mine bringing me here, because I will never have anything to say to you.'

There was a taut silence. 'You think?' he said finally. '"Never" might be beyond even you.' He stared down at her, the overhead lights carving shadows beneath his cheekbones. 'And if you're thinking about running away—don't. There's no point. It's a twenty-eight-hour hike across the dunes to the city.'

She could feel her heart banging high and hard somewhere beneath her ribs. 'Sounds like a dream compared to spending another minute with you.'

His eyes narrowed, but he didn't rise to her words. Instead, he seemed to expand the space, and anger and panic and misery and exhaustion reared inside her like the four horsemen of the apocalypse, and she slammed her open palms against his chest.

'Get out. Go on. *Get out.*'

She breathed in sharply as his hands caught her wrists, and for what felt like several lifetimes she struggled against him as he stood staring down at her, deliberate and unflinching. Then, without saying a word, he let go of her, turned, and stalked out of the room, closing the door softly behind him.

Heart still pounding, she waited for the click of a key, but he didn't lock the door.

But then he didn't need to.

Suddenly, as if she had been running too fast, her legs started to shake. She sat down on the bed, staring blindly around the room. Large and square with pale walls and whisper-light muslin curtains, its only colour came from a huge Persian rug.

It was beautiful.

A quick, violent tremor rippled through her as she remembered Omar saying this place had been a fortress. Now it was a prison—the most beautiful, elegant prison in the world. And she was locked in here with her pain, trapped with her anger, and her misery, and a man who hated her almost as much as she hated herself.

Stalking away from Delphi's beautiful, pale, defiant face, Omar walked straight past his own room. There was no point going to bed. He wasn't going to sleep. He needed space… he needed air—

He needed to go back in time.

Back to before he had decided to take up Dan's invitation to play polo at the Amersham. Back to when Delphi Wright Howard had been just a name in the ether.

Breathing out unsteadily, he ran lightly up a narrow staircase and pushed open a door. His heartbeat juddering through his bones, he stared up into the inky blackness of the sky, his brain automatically joining up the stars to form constellations.

If only it was as easy to make sense of his wife.

But she was out of reach as Orion's belt.

What if she'd stayed pregnant? What then?

He thought back to the small, warm weight of Khalid in his arms, then switched effortlessly to an image of Delphi, gazing down not at Khalid but at another dark-eyed, soft-skinned baby.

It was too much to bear. It was easier to focus on how she had left him in the dark. To fix on the anger and pain of being the last to know when he should have been the first.

He glanced up at the sky, his chest aching. The moon was still watching him, just as it had been back in the city.

'Thanks for the help,' he muttered.

But he couldn't blame the moon. Delphi was a force of nature in her own right.

And he was an Emirati, he thought with a stab of pride. His people had conquered nature to build a city that was the envy of the world. Surely he could conquer one woman?

Feeling calmer, he made his way back downstairs. The building was still and quiet, but as he walked past Delphi's closed bedroom door his footsteps faltered. He thought he had heard a noise…faint like the whispering sand on the dunes.

It must be the wind.

He thought back to the still, night air, his chest tightening.

It wasn't the wind.

He opened the door, his breath knotting in his throat as the shadows darted across the room. On the bed, still in her beautiful dress, Delphi was moaning in her sleep, her face creased in distress, her hands clutching the bedspread.

CHAPTER SIX

'THREE... FOUR... FIVE...'

Delphi ran lightly through the ranch house. She felt happy and free and excited. Hide and seek was her favourite game.

Ed would find Scott first. Her middle brother was too laid-back to bother hiding properly. Will was way better, but she was the best.

And the smallest.

Except she wasn't small anymore. She stared down confusedly at her body in a glittering golden gown. When did that happen?

'Six... Seven... Eight...'

The hairs on the back of her neck rose. Behind her, Ed's voice was fading. Across the room, the familiar stone fireplace was collapsing, the walls dissolving to mist, and now she was in an overgrown graveyard, standing in front of a lipstick-covered headstone.

Heart drumming against her ribs, she forced down a scream and stumbled backwards, star-

ing wildly in every direction. Her skin was burning as if she had caught the sun, but the mist was chillingly cold. She could hear other voices now, different, unfamiliar, rising and falling, drawing nearer on every side. They sounded harsh; they sounded hungry, and she knew she had to get away.

Run, she told herself. As fast as you can.

Only it wasn't her speaking, but Dan.

'Nine... Ten... Here, I come. Ready or not...' the voice chanted, close by now.

Whimpering, she spun away, slipping sideways, brambles clawing at her dress, but she couldn't run because she was holding a baby: she was holding Khalid.

She stared down into his liquid, dark eyes, waves of hot slippery panic surging over her skin. Around her, the mist was closing in, growing brighter, sharpening into a flash of light, then another, and another.

'Ianthe, this way—'

'Over here, Dylan—'

The voices were getting louder...the light was dizzying, swallowing her up.

She felt her grip loosen, felt Khalid start to slip from her fingers. She opened her mouth, and the sound of screaming filled her head...

'Delphi! Delphi, it's okay.'

Another voice, this time close by.

Her eyes snapped open, and she jerked upright, gasping, breathless, arms flailing, snatching for the baby. But he wasn't there.

'Khalid... Khalid...' She croaked his name, her body rigid, shuddering with fear and panic, and then a hand touched her arm and she lashed out wildly.

'Delphi, it's okay. You're okay.'

Omar was leaning over her, the outline of his body blurred in the moonlight filtering through the half-closed curtains. After the dizzying blaze of lights in her dream the soft darkness felt surreal and, inching up the bed, she stared past him, her heart still pounding, trying to make sense of her surroundings, and then she remembered.

'What are you doing?' She tried to clear her throat from the last of her panic. 'Why are you here?'

'I was walking past your door, and I heard you.' He hesitated just for a second. 'I heard a noise. I just wanted to check that you were okay.'

Okay? She let out a shaky breath, somewhere between a choke and sob. She had lost their baby. Her heart was broken. And her marriage was over. She doubted anything would ever be okay again.

'I'm fine,' she lied.

Actually, she felt exhausted, and horribly cold that she was having to hold herself rigid not to shake. But then she was still wearing her dress and evening sandals.

'You didn't sound fine.'

'It's nothing. I just had a dream.'

His face was in shadow, but she could sense his uncertainty—and something else. Something that felt horribly like concern. Only she couldn't let herself think like that. Couldn't let herself believe that Omar cared about her.

She thought back to the moment in the garden when he had reached out and touched her hand, and she had weakened, leaning into him, and just like that she had got used to the feel of his body against hers, to his solidity and his gentleness. She could have stayed there in his arms for ever, letting his heat and strength envelop her.

But it was dangerous to think like that. Or rather it was dangerous to stop thinking and let her body make the decisions.

She felt his gaze on her face. 'It sounded more like a nightmare to me,' he said quietly.

Remembering the mist and the gravestone, she felt her hands start to shake, and she flattened them against the mattress to steady herself. It had been so long since she'd had that nightmare and she'd forgotten the horror of it, the horror of the aftermath too.

'It's nothing,' she said again, trying to sound normal…casual, even. Only it didn't feel like nothing, and suddenly she wanted him to hold her more than she had ever wanted anything in life.

And so, of course, she had to make him leave.

'Really, it's nothing. You don't need to worry about me. Honestly. Just go and get some sleep.'

He stared at her in silence, his face unreadable, and then without a word, he turned and walked out of the room. She let out a shuddering breath. Without Omar there she didn't have to hold back anymore, and her body started to shiver uncontrollably.

She had opened the window earlier and now she thought about shutting it—only that would mean moving and she wasn't sure her legs were working. Instead, she drew her knees to her chest and hugged them, lowering her face so as not to have to look into the unfamiliar corners of the room.

She should have been relieved that he was gone, but instead she wanted to turn and weep into her pillow. She shouldn't have let him go. She should have asked him to stay. She should have tried to talk to him—

Tears filled her eyes.

No, it was better this way.

But if that was true, then why did it hurt so much? Why had having him there made her feel so much want and need and hope?

'Here.'

She glanced up. Omar was holding out a glass with a measure of clear golden liquid. His dark eyes rested on her face and her breath caught. He was still so much a part of her, and she wondered helplessly if that feeling would ever gentle. Would the ache of losing him ever stop?

'It's brandy.' He paused. 'I know you said you didn't want a drink earlier, but it might help now.'

She had been about to refuse, only his face in the moonlight looked soft, younger, as he must have looked when he was little, and she felt something twist inside her as she imagined how their child might have looked had he been a boy.

Forcing her mind away from that devastating train of thought, she took the glass. 'Thank you.'

Brandy wasn't something she would usually drink, but it was what people drank on TV and in films when they were in shock, so maybe it would help her stop feeling so cold.

'You're shaking.' Frowning, he reached down and touched her arm, then her cheek. 'You're freezing.'

His skin felt blissfully warm, and she had to stop herself from rubbing her face against his fingers like a cat. But it was the gentleness in his voice that made her want to take his hand and wrap it round her waist like a bandage.

Not wanting him to feel that need in her, she got to her feet. 'I should probably get changed.'

She just about managed to totter into the bathroom. But once she had closed the door, the energy that had propelled her there evaporated. Even the thought of getting undressed seemed almost unimaginably complicated, and her fingers were so numb she couldn't even feel the buttons, much less tackle the thin leather straps of her sandals.

But finally, after a few false starts, she managed to undress herself.

It was only then, standing naked apart from a pair of flesh-coloured panties, that she remembered she didn't have anything to change into.

There was a knock at the door.

'Would these be of any use?'

She opened it a crack. Omar was holding out a pile of clothes. Men's clothes—presumably his.

'They'll be a little big, but they should be warm.'

They *were* big. She had to roll up the legs and the waistband of the loose cotton trousers several times, and the T-shirt looked more like a mini dress. But they were soft and warm.

Omar was sitting on the bed as she came into the room, and he watched in silence as she carefully laid her dress on the armchair by the window. As she turned, he stood up, and she felt her stomach lurch.

She had half expected him to still be there when she finally walked back into the bedroom. What she hadn't expected was the fierce, chaotic rush of relief, and for a few half-seconds she fought the same urge as earlier, to step into the circle of his arms and let him hold her close as he had in the garden.

But she couldn't just hand herself over to him again. It had been so hard to trust him the first time and leaving him had been brutal. She wasn't about to start up that whole cycle again. Only the flipside of that was that she couldn't expect him to comfort her either.

The bed was still warm from where he had been sitting and she wriggled under the covers. In a moment she would tell him to go, but it wouldn't matter if he stayed for a few moments longer, she told herself. Just until the nightmare faded a bit more.

'Here.'

He handed her the brandy again. Her fingers brushed against his as she took the glass, and she felt the contact like an electric current. Only how could such an impersonal touch make her feel like that?

The answer to that question made her panic so much that she wanted to bolt down the brandy in one frantic gulp. But she didn't. They were over. Her mind was straight about that, and she didn't need alcohol un-straightening it.

'Are you not having one?' she asked.

He shook his head. 'I'm not the one who had a nightmare.'

Except he had, in a way, she thought, remembering his shocked expression when she'd told him about the miscarriage. He just hadn't been asleep.

'I'm sorry about the party. I'll write to your parents…tell them it was my fault we left early.' She gave him a small, tight smile. 'They're going to hate me soon enough anyway. Your whole family will.'

And it shouldn't matter, but it did. She thought about Jalila taking her hands. She had been so open and welcoming. They might have been friends—like sisters, even. But now that was ruined too, before it had even started.

His eyes rested on her face. 'Why would they hate you?'

'Because I'm divorcing their son, their brother, their uncle.'

Picturing Khalid in his arms was almost enough to unloose the emotion trapped inside her, and she took a shaky sip of the brandy. It was smooth and rich and complex—a bit like the man who had handed it to her, she thought, glancing up at Omar.

While she'd been in the bathroom he had switched on a lamp by the bed and its light was spilling across the room, chasing away the dark shadows in the corners. And now that there was more light, she could see his face clearly.

Her heart began beating faster. His dark eyes looked smudged, and there was a tension in his shoulders as if he was holding some invisible weight.

'You look tired,' she said quietly. Actually, he looked exhausted.

'There's been a lot going on.'

'You mean work.'

There had been a hint of bitterness in her voice, and she knew from the tiny, defensive flash in his eyes that he had heard it. But there was no trace of anger or pent-up frustration in his tone when he replied. Instead, there was a rough edge that hurt, high up between her ribs.

'Work. Planning the party. But mostly trying to find you.'

His beautiful face was taut.

'I don't know which was worse. Being told you were in hospital. That you'd been in a car accident. Or finding out about the baby.'

She thought back to the moment when she'd told him about the pregnancy and the miscarriage. They hadn't been touching, but she had still felt the physical impact of those two statements on Omar. Now the pain in his eyes knifed through her.

'And then hearing you cry out like that—'

He broke off and walked towards the window, his head tilting up towards the moon, hovering serenely in the blue-black darkness.

Delphi stared at his profile. She didn't know what to do...what to say. Normally, she was the one who retreated into herself, and the more questions Omar asked the deeper she retreated, the longer her silences. But now, for the first time in her life, she was the one wanting to break the stillness in the room.

'It was just a bad dream. I used to have them when I was younger, sometimes.'

His face turned towards her. 'After the crash, you mean?'

She nodded slowly. 'Yes, but they didn't start immediately—more like six months later. Apparently, it's very common with very young children who lose a parent.' She drew in a breath. 'Parents… The grief counsellor said it was my way of coming to terms with what had happened.'

Her legs were trembling again.

'I used to get really panicky about going to bed. Dan tried loads of different things. A nightlight…warm, milky drinks. But what worked in the end was him sleeping on the floor by my bed.'

Like some faithful hound. She could see Dan's face. Outwardly calm, reassuring, unfazed. But beneath the patient, soothing smile he'd been exhausted. Shattered by grief and regret and the need to do his best for her even though she wasn't his child.

'He did that every night,' she said quietly. 'Even though it went on for quite a long time… maybe a year. Always the same dream.'

There was another silence.

'Apart from tonight?'

His voice was so low she might have missed his question. She stared at him, her heart beating unevenly. 'Why do you say that?'

He hesitated, as if he was debating something. Then, 'You were shouting Khalid's name.

But you obviously hadn't met him until this evening, so you must have been having a different nightmare.'

His words fluttered up towards the moon like moths.

'It started off the same.' She swallowed, reluctant to go back to the beginning, knowing what was to follow. 'I'm playing hide and seek with my brothers. It was my favourite game. I was always the best at hiding.'

She half expected Omar to make some facetious remark, but he said nothing.

'I'm in the ranch house. Only then the house collapses and there's this mist…' She shivered. 'It's cold, and then I realise I'm in a graveyard. I can't hear Ed counting any more, but there are other voices. And then the mist gets brighter and brighter, and I know it's the men with the cameras. The men who camped outside my parents' house for days…'

Gazing down at Delphi, Omar felt sick to his stomach. His heart felt as if it was going to break through his ribs. So intensely it took his breath away, he wanted to reach out and touch her small, stiff body, to pull her close until that pain in her face melted away.

She had never talked about the days following her parents' accident, and even now she was only doing so obliquely, by telling him about her dream. But he knew how much she feared the paparazzi, and the efforts she had made her whole life to avoid coming to their attention.

A beat of anger pulsed across his skin. He hated it that they still cornered her when she was at her most vulnerable. Asleep, and trapped in a nightmare from which there was no escape.

'What happens next?' he said quietly.

'That's when I start running.'

His chest tightened. A year before they'd met, two years ago now, Delphi had gone to Wyoming to help tag the wild horses. He could still remember her face, that mix of envy and empathy, as she'd told him about the trip. About how some of the mustangs had refused to be caught. How they would keep running, their pounding hooves filling the air with dust.

Delphi had been running since she was four years old. In one way or another she hadn't ever stopped running. First from the paparazzi. From her scandalous past and her fear of being hurt. Then from him and the wreck of their marriage.

'And I try to run,' she went on. 'Only I can't because I'm holding Khalid, and I'm scared I'll trip.'

Omar stared down at her, his pulse jerking. When she had been in the bathroom he had switched on the light, sensing that it would comfort her. Now, though, the air in the room had gone dark with the sadness and pain of her past.

Her mouth trembled. 'And then the mist starts to swallow me up and I can't see my hands.'

He saw the flash of pain in her eyes, the panic.

'I can't feel them. And then I let go of Khalid. I let go of him—'

She made a small, wordless noise and pressed her hand not against her mouth, but in front of her stomach, just as she had back in the garden, and he moved then, crossing the room in three strides, putting his arms around her and pulling her close.

Her head was on his shoulder, and she was sobbing, and he didn't try to stop her. He knew she was crying for another baby. A baby that she would never press close to her beating heart.

His chest tightened. He had wanted this for so long. Wanted her to confide in him…wanted her to need him and only him. And now he had what he wanted. Only he felt no satisfaction or triumph. Instead, he felt suddenly and savagely angry with himself. What kind of man would want his wife to be so diminished and desperate?

His own eyes burning, he stroked her hair, speaking softly in Arabic, saying the words his mother had used whenever he'd fallen and hurt his knee. The same words she had spoken whenever his father had left early one morning without saying goodbye.

He felt her breathe out shakily and he shifted backwards on the bed, taking her with him, tucking the covers over her trembling body. Still stroking her hair, he said softly, 'You didn't let go of our baby, Delphi. If there was anything you could have done to hold on to it, you would have done.'

She was shaking her head. 'I should never have gone back to England.'

He could feel her fighting for control, fighting to stay calm. It had caught him off guard, her deciding to go. He'd known England wasn't a happy place for her—and not just because it was where her childhood had ended. After her parents' deaths, Dylan Wright's sisters had each tried to get custody of their niece, arguing that, unlike Dan, they were blood relatives. Dan had won, but it had been a long, vitriolic battle, played out in the tabloid press, and the media attention had got worse and worse.

The final straw had come when stories about

Delphi had appeared online. It had been clear that the 'sources close to the family' quoted were people she had trusted. It was then that Dan had moved her to the ranch house.

Dan, the cuckolded husband, and substitute father had upended his world to make his wife's daughter feel safe. No wonder Delphi trusted him.

'Your father thought it was a good idea,' he said quietly.

She looked up at him, her eyes wide with shock. 'How do you know that?'

'I called him. When I got back from Sydney. After you changed your mind again about going.' He hesitated. Then, 'I was worried. You were distracted. Preoccupied.' *Like his father.* As always, that had been his first thought. 'I told him I thought you should forget about going, but Dan said you needed to go.'

His chest felt tight. *'She's scared of what she's going to feel,'* Dan had told him. *'And when she's scared, she pushes things and people away. And she's been pushing the past away forever.'* There had been sadness in the older man's voice. *'I want to help her, only I can't—because I'm part of the problem, part of that past. But you...you're her future. So go with her, help her face the past and let her live the life she deserves.'*

A wave of self-loathing rose up inside him. Because he hadn't gone with her, had he? He had gone to meet Bob Maclean.

'I know he wanted me to go. He tried so many times to make it happen,' Delphi said in a small, bruised voice. 'One year, we got all the way to the airport.'

The twist to the corner of her mouth told him that was as far as they'd got.

His throat was dry. 'So what was different about this time?'

She bit down on the inside of her lip. 'You.' Her beautiful brown eyes flicked to his face, then away. 'And then the pregnancy.' Her breathing was suddenly unsteady again. 'I really was going to tell you, but when I found out you were in Sydney, and I wanted to do it face to face. So I decided to wait.'

She glanced up at him, and in the light from the bedside lamp she looked soft-edged…like a painting.

'Only the whole time I kept thinking about going to London. It was just there, in the back of my mind. And then I realised why. I realised that I wanted to tell them too. My parents, I mean. I wanted us all to be there together. But then everything went wrong.'

Her words fell into silence.

'You said you couldn't come. I should have

told you then, only I was angry with you, so I didn't. The whole flight over I felt odd, and then when I reached the graveyard it got worse. I thought it was just nerves and excitement.'

Hearing the echo of that excitement in her voice, Omar felt his heart squeeze tight. He knew all about that jittery anticipation; that mix of hope and tension. His father's absences and returns had governed his life like the rising and setting of the sun. He could still remember all the days and sometimes weeks when Rashid had been away on business or staying at his other homes.

Everything around him had felt flimsy and makeshift…like scenery on a stage. His mother had always been breathless and on edge, like an actor waiting in the wings for her cue. And he had been a small, fearful boy, sitting like some sentinel by the window overlooking the driveway, scared both that Rashid would never return or, worse, that when he did, he would look right straight through his youngest child without even seeing him.

He felt a rush of shame. At least he had a father and a mother.

He stared down at Delphi's small, tense body. 'You'd waited so long to go there,' he said gently.

There was no excitement in her face now.

Just pain. ‘Long enough to realise that maybe another day would be a better idea. It’s not like it was some tradition I had to keep. I mean, I’d managed to miss the anniversary of their deaths every other year.’

His eyes didn’t leave her face, but he barely heard her words. Instead, that static was roaring in his ears again, and something that had been fluttering like moths’ wings at the edges of the mind was suddenly there centre-stage, clear and sharp in the spotlight. She had lost their baby on the same date she had lost her parents all those years ago.

He made himself speak. ‘You couldn’t have known the paparazzi would be there.’

Her face was paper-white. ‘Couldn’t I? They’d never left my parents alone in life—why should it have been any different when they were dead?’

She glanced past him to where a thin straight line of light was quivering along the horizon. It was the dawn of a new day—but not for Delphi. She was still reliving those hours alone in London.

‘The cramping started on my way back to the apartment. When I got there, I went to the bathroom, and that’s when I realised I was bleeding. I should have gone to the hospital, but I was too scared to move. And I thought if I stayed still the bleeding would stop.'

His hands tightened in her hair. He didn't want to think about her bleeding, in pain, scared. *Alone.* Would the outcome have been different if he'd been there? Probably not. He knew that miscarriage was common...

And that's relevant, how?

The question was an angry roar inside his head. He was her husband. She had needed his support, needed him to be there. Instead, he'd been chasing another deal.

He thought back to the meeting with Maclean. Or rather the meetings, plural. Hours and hours spent picking through the contract with his lawyers while he'd been fighting jet lag and a need for Delphi that had crept into every fibre of his being, so that simple activities like brushing his teeth and getting dressed had felt impossible.

And what did he have to show for it? Another cable network in Australia.

But what if he had been there with Delphi?

Would it have been different?

It was the second time he'd asked himself that question, and he wanted the answer to be definite. He needed it to be no, but he wasn't sure it was. He didn't know if he would ever be sure.

Only he couldn't deal with that now. Right now, Delphi needed him, and this time he wasn't going to let her down.

'You did the right thing.'

She looked up at him. Her eyes were puffy, her cheeks tearstained. 'Did I? I just keep going over all the things I could have done.'

The static was roaring in the ears again.

'You can't think like that. Miscarriages happen for all kinds of reasons.'

She was shaking her head. 'I know. But I was so sure it was going to be okay. Everything's always been so difficult for me. School. Making friends. Even you.' Her voice shook a little. 'But this was so easy. I was just pregnant. No fuss. No drama. And I thought that must mean something. But it was the same. I couldn't make it work.'

In the dimly lit room, her body was made of shadows.

'I'm so tired of having to fight for everything… I can't do it any more…'

The ache in her voice rolled over him like one of the sandstorms that swept in from the desert, and he heard it then. Not just grief, but defeat, and finally he understood that she had lost more than their baby in London. What little faith she'd ever had in him, and in the world and in herself, had been torn from her.

His arms tightened around her, and guilt swelled inside his chest, crushing his lungs so that it was difficult to take a breath.

'And you don't have to. You're not alone, Delphi. I'm right here, and I'm not going anywhere.'

He held her close, cradling her against his body, stroking her hair, wishing he had more than words to prove what he was saying.

He didn't know how long they stayed locked together. Maybe they would have stayed there all night but somewhere in the night an owl screeched and she shifted away from him, blinking as if she had woken from a trance.

Staring up at Omar, Delphi felt her heart flutter. She knew that to stay any longer in the half-circle of his arm was a risk not worth taking, but already she missed his hand caressing her hair, gentle as the wings of a hummingbird.

'You should probably go and get some sleep. Goodness knows what time it is…'

'Is that what you want?' he asked.

His eyes were fixed on hers, dark and velvet-soft, shimmering with something that made her breath catch and her heart feel suddenly too big for her chest. She had supposed that talking would unravel the last threads binding them together. But how could 'we' become 'I' when he was holding her so close? Suddenly she was acutely aware of the thin layers of fabric that was all there was between her skin and his.

'Do you want me to leave?'

She felt her body tense in objection. But her body was not to be trusted. She was not to be trusted. 'I want… I want…' She paused, took a breath, tried again. 'I want…'

There was a beat of silence.

Her heart was speeding now, and she knew she should push him away, but she was hypnotised by the sudden harshness of his breathing. Around them the lights were blurring and the air in the room was changing, blooming, starting to press in on them, weighty with the feelings they had both pushed aside—feelings she refused to name but that were impossible to ignore, impossible to deny.

'I want it too,' he said hoarsely.

A minute went by, and then another. And then, reaching up, she touched his cheek, tracing the line of his mouth with her thumb, fear and desire and anticipation chasing through her restless body. Somewhere in the back of her mind a drum was beating out a panicky, percussive message in Morse code.

Stop this. Stop this now.

But it was too late. Her heart was beating louder. Running wild and free like a mustang across the sagebrush grasslands. She wanted him. Wanted the kiss. And now she leaned into him and brushed her lips against his. Her belly clenched with desire as their warm breath mingled, and then their mouths met blindly, fiercely. Any thoughts she had of stopping were forgotten, all doubts and memories and pain dropping away as the taste of him went straight to her head and there was nothing but his solid body and his warm breath.

She felt his hand move to her cheek, the callused thumb stroking the soft skin there. This was right, she thought, feeling the heat beneath the light caress. This was what mattered.

Heat flared inside her as his fingers slid from her cheek, down over her collarbone to cup her breast. A galaxy of tiny stars exploded inside her head as his fingertips grazed the nipple. She twitched, muscles tightening. Heat was flooding her limbs, dissolving her body, and she felt the kiss change, felt him change.

Lips parting, her breath quickening, she could feel his heart, feel his pulse beating into her body. His mouth was moving against hers, shaping her desire, and then he shifted her weight, tipping her forward, and she felt the hard press of his erection against her pelvis.

He took a quick breath, like a gasp, and she arched helplessly into his groin, breasts aching, a shivery pleasure dancing through her veins as he forced her head up, deepening the kiss, sliding his hands beneath her top to find hot, bare skin. Touching, teasing, tormenting…

Closing her eyes, she rested her forehead against his. Oh, how she had missed him… missed this. This was what she needed. He was what she needed. Only Omar could do this. Only he could feed the hunger and soothe this tenderness in her chest, soothe this ache that felt like a huge, dark bruise swallowing up her heart.

'*Delphi*... Stop, we have to stop…'

Her eyes opened. The carousel was slowing. Omar's hands were on her shoulders, his thumbs gripping her collarbone.

Breath snagged in her chest and something like a sob rose in her throat. She was fighting him, trying to pull him closer, her mouth seeking his, her body not fully under her control, and she realised with shock that her face was wet with tears.

'Shh…' he said soothingly. His hands were gentle, but he was holding her firmly. 'You've been so brave, so strong. Let me take care of you.' As her body went limp, he clasped her face, thumbs stroking the tears from her cheeks. 'It's okay.'

He tipped her gently off his lap onto the bed

and she lay down, feeling suddenly, brutally tired.

'It's okay,' he said again, tucking the covers around her body and lying down next to her.

His hand was moving gently through her hair, like the breeze through the woods that surrounded the ranch house.

'You're not alone, Delphi. I'm right here, and I'm not going anywhere. You can sleep now.'

Sometime later, Delphi stirred. She felt warm and safe, just as she had as a child but as her eyes fluttered open, she saw not Dan but Omar sprawled in the armchair, her dress clutched in his arms, his head resting awkwardly in the crook of his arm.

She knew she was dreaming, but it was still calming to see him there, and for a moment she watched the rise and fall of his chest, feeling the rhythm of his breath inside her own body. And then her eyes closed again, and sleep pulled her back under.

CHAPTER SEVEN

PUSHING OPEN THE WINDOWS, Delphi took a step back from the punch of heat. It felt as if the air was on fire. She had woken late, and it had taken her a moment or two to orientate herself, then another longer moment to process everything that had happened in the hours following the party. Coming here to the mountains, fighting with Omar again, that twisted nightmare involving Khalid and her parents, and then, finally, talking to him about the miscarriage.

Raising an arm to shield her face, she breathed out shakily. It was a conversation she had never expected to have with him. Like so many other conversations in her life, she had let the weight of it carry it down to the depths of her mind. Only somehow, last night, it had come bubbling up to the surface.

Her face trembled in the sunlight. She hadn't cried since those few terrible hours when she'd realised she was losing their baby—but then she wasn't a crier. She never had been. She had learned early on that tears had no power to change the things you didn't like.

But last night she had cried—sobbed, in fact, in Omar's arms. For her parents. Her marriage. The baby she would never hold. For the failures of her life. For the failure she was.

Only after she had stopped crying things had changed.

The pain had still been there, but distant, softer, so that it no longer hurt to swallow or breathe—almost as if some of the jagged edges inside her had been rubbed smooth.

And it wasn't just about her talking.

Omar had listened.

Instead of pushing her for answers, or boxing her in like before, he had given her space, let her set the pace. It had still been hard for her to get the words out, but for the first time in their relationship she hadn't felt like an item on his agenda to be ticked off, or a challenge to be overcome and conquered.

He had treated her in a different way, and because he'd been different—quieter, less intense—things had taken a different path and she had finally managed to open up to him. Not just about the dates and the places. She had shared her feelings. And it had been painful and exhausting and terrifying to relive those hours, but somehow not to have done so would have been a worse option, and that was a first too.

And after all the talk and the tears she had slept deeply.

But not dreamlessly.

She glanced back into the room at the armchair. Last night, in her dreams, Omar had slept in that chair, his muscular body contorted into the velvet upholstery, her dress hugged tight in his arms. And when not keeping watch on her he had slipped into bed beside her, pulling her against him, their bodies blurring as her hands had splayed over his shoulders, his hands parting her thighs, his tongue dipping inside her with tortuous precision—

All dreams.

Only it was hard to remember that when she could almost feel of him holding her against him as if nothing had ever gone wrong between them. Feel them both moving as one, to touch, to kiss, to pull closer, kiss deeper. His mouth, her mouth, his hands, her fingers…all seeking the same goal with the same urgency.

And it didn't matter that it was nonsense for it to have still been like that between them. In her dream she had felt him lose control, heard that sharp intake of breath when he'd tipped her into his lap against the hard ridge of his erection. And her body had responded instantly, instinctively. Softening and flowing towards him. The barriers she had created between them melting like winter ice in spring sunshine.

Only as much as it had felt right, it had been wrong. Because there had been loss and loneliness and sadness mixed in with the lust. Not that she had noticed or cared. She'd been racing towards the edge of the abyss…

It had been Omar who had pulled back from the brink—pulled them both back from the brink. She should be grateful for that. And part of her was.

She glanced down at the 'wedding ring' Omar had given her in the car on the way to the party.

Why, then, did she feel as if her heart was breaking all over again?

At some point while she'd slept her suitcase had been delivered to her room, and she dressed in the dress she had been wearing in Idaho and a pair of flat sandals. It felt strange, putting it back on.

She glanced down at the fluttering fabric as she left the bedroom. Was it really only three days since she'd been at that Fourth of July barbecue?

Now, that was the kind of simple yes/no question she could answer.

The other question—the one about her

heart— required not just thought but a mental agility that was a stretch for her right now. She knew she had hurt Omar, and even though he had hurt her, by continually failing to put her first, she cared that he was hurt. And she knew he cared that she was hurt too.

'You're not alone, Delphi. I'm right here, and I'm not going anywhere.'

It would be so easy to believe Omar meant what he'd said, to let his words catch fire inside her. But she knew that it was the kind of thing people said in the moment before they had sex. The kind of thing estranged couples said before make-up sex.

Except they hadn't had sex.

Her footsteps faltered. Was this the right way?

Arriving last night, it had been dark, and she had been too furious to take in her surroundings, but none of this felt familiar. She walked a little bit further and then stopped, pressing her hand against the wall to steady herself. There was a door only half open, but thanks to the beautiful, antique cot she could see she knew that she was looking at a nursery.

Her heart pounding inside her head, she stepped into the room. It was a tiny oasis of palest green, with a canopy of exotic hand-painted flowers trailing from the ceiling that looked just like the ones outside their honeymoon suite in Maui. Her eyes tracked slowly around the room. There was a photograph of Las Vegas and another of some grazing horses—no, not just some horses…

She took a step closer, her breath catching.

They were *her* horses: Embla and The Pigeon.

She turned slowly on the spot. Last night, Omar had made it sound as if this fort was a new acquisition. Or maybe she had just heard it that way. But it couldn't be, she thought, as her gaze moved from a lamp with a Statue-of-Liberty-shaped base to the Roman blinds decorated with pictures of caravans of camels. Every detail had been carefully chosen as a reminder of the places that were unique and special to the two of them.

Eyes burning, she dug her fingers into the back of a pink velvet sofa.

For so long she had thought Omar indifferent, but now, standing here, thinking about him creating this for her…for the child he'd imagined them having one day…she felt the thread that had come loose inside her last night begin to unravel a little more.

The thread unravelled again as she made her way through the rooms downstairs. Despite having only arrived last night, she felt strangely at home in a way that she never had in the slick, modern interior of their New York apartment. Maybe because this was more like the Bedford ranch house in feel, with huge, faded rugs, exposed stone walls and comfortable linen-covered sofas.

Outside on a terrace, breakfast—or perhaps brunch—was set out beneath a huge cream canopy. She sat down, realising as she did so that for the first time in weeks, she felt hungry. Ravenous, in fact. And that wasn't the only change. It seemed easier to breathe than it had been yesterday. But maybe that was just the mountain air.

The food was delicious.

Puffy melt-in-the-mouth flatbreads with fennel, cardamom and saffron. Scrambled eggs cooked with vermicelli rice, caramelised onions, raisins and rose water—and, of course, dates and coffee.

But she was too distracted by the view to fully concentrate on what she was eating. In the dark, the mountains had been simply shapes. Now, though, they rose grey-brown, majestic, and implacable, and so huge that the fort looked like a child's toy. It was impossible not to be impressed. The garden, too, was impressive—not just in scale but in its lush greenness. All palm trees quivering in the heat and verdant lawns broken up by narrow, vibrantly coloured tiled pools.

It was like an oasis, she thought—and instantly she was back upstairs in that pale jewel of a nursery.

She could have sat there for what remained of the morning, trying to make sense of that tiny green room, and maybe she would have done if she hadn't heard the sound of something so irresistibly familiar that her limbs were moving of their own accord, and she was pushing back her chair to investigate.

Heart pounding, she followed the sound to a dark oak door. Walking through it, she pressed her hand against the wall to steady herself. She had found the stables. Her breath caught and, feeling a buzz of excitement and impatience, she walked towards where horses were peering over their half-doors, whickering and stamping.

'Hello, my beauty,' she said softly to the grey in the nearest stall.

The horse responded, leaning forward to rest its face against hers, and, closing her eyes, she breathed in the smell of straw and leather and sweat.

'I thought I might find you here.'

Her eyes snapped open. Omar was standing at the entrance to the stables, watching her intently, his muscular shoulder wedged against the door frame. She hadn't actually allowed herself to think about this moment, but after her febrile X-rated dreams it was a shock to see him looking calm, composed, and fully clothed in worn-in white twill jeans, jodhpur boots and the faded blue and yellow Howard Harriers polo shirt, worn by her father's polo team.

That gave her a jolt, and she wondered momentarily why he was wearing that particular shirt. There were any number of possible answers to that question, all equally unnerving, but luckily, he chose that moment to walk towards her, and all thought was drowned out by the sound of her heart hammering like a blacksmith shoeing a horse.

'I'm sorry. I shouldn't have just let myself in.'

'I'm glad you did.' He inclined his head towards the mare. 'Her name's Alima. It means wise.'

She watched him stroke the horse's neck, his fingers moving slowly and steadily over the silky coat and felt her pulse jumping haphazardly like a startled frog. Omar had a great sense of touch, and it was far too easy to remember those strong, firm hands caressing her body, effortlessly making her soft and hot, making her melt inside.

'And is she?' she asked, turning away, hoping that nothing of what she was thinking had shown on her face. 'Wise, I mean?'

'She is. But she's also young, and she doesn't trust very easily. Her last owner messed up her head, so you get one chance and then she tries to buck you off. And if that fails, she bolts.'

She glanced up at him sharply, sensing something beneath his words, but his face was smooth and unreadable.

'That's a pity.' It was none of her business, but she couldn't stop herself from asking, 'And what's her current owner doing about that?'

His eyes didn't leave her face. 'Honestly? He's struggling a little.'

Fine lines fanned out from the corners of his eyes, and she felt a click of connection between them. Trying to ignore it, she said, 'Any particular reason?'

'I think she requires a sensitivity and lightness of touch that's beyond him.'

Her nipples tightened against her dress as he reached past her and picked up the head collar hanging from a hook outside the loose box. They were standing far too close, and she had a sudden, sharp flashback to the moment last night when she'd leaned in and brushed her mouth against his.

'How old is she?'

'Two,' he said softly.

She watched, dry-mouthed, as his hand slid up and over Alima's beautiful muzzle. Above the scent of horse sweat and hay, she caught a whisper of his scent—that mix of skin and salt and sage that made all the air leave her body.

He unbolted the stable door and led Alima out onto the flagstones, and as he walked the horse in small circles she saw instantly what he meant. There was a tension in the way the mare was moving, an uncertainty in her step that made Delphi's fingers itch to smooth the twitches from the horse's quivering flank.

'Any thoughts?'

Glancing up, she met Omar's gaze. She felt that feverish embrace swell up in her again—not just as a memory but tangible, so that she could feel his mouth, his hands, on her skin.

Flushed with panicky heat, she opened her mouth, fully intending to tell him that she would email him the name of several equine therapists who might help, and that now she wanted to leave.

Only instead she found herself saying, 'Do you have any boots I can borrow?'

There was a sand school next to the stables and, watching Alima trotting alongside the post and rail fencing, she forgot about Omar, forgot about leaving the fort. All her attention was focused on the little horse.

She was a beautiful animal, but her her tail was clamped in tight. A bird suddenly screamed high up in the sky and Alima shot forward, her eyes rolling white, but Delphi kept her moving, waiting until the horse's movements softened, and then she let Alima come to a standstill.

'There you go, little one,' she murmured, letting the horse sniff her hand.

Breathing softly, she waited until Alima gave a whicker of consent, and then she moved her hand slowly to the horse's neck, working her way along the mare's body. As she moved, she kept talking…nothing that mattered or made any sense, just talking softly.

Watching Delphi lean into the horse, Omar felt his heart slow. Last night, just for a few hours, it was as if the past seven weeks had never happened. She had fallen asleep in his arms, the way they'd always slept.

Asleep, it was the one time when she would relax her guard and let him get close to her.

Aside from when they made love.

Jaw clenching, he pushed that thought away, just as he had pushed Delphi away on the bed. He wasn't ready to go there yet. Instead, he thought back to her face, pale in the lamplight, and the tremor in her voice as she'd told him what he wanted to know. What he'd thought he wanted to know.

His fingers tightened against the railing. He hated picturing her curled up on that cold bathroom floor in London. But it was the exhaustion in her voice that still haunted him.

Waking at dawn in the armchair, with the daylight pressing redly against his eyelids, he'd had a stiff neck and a head full of questions, the answers to which should have been irrelevant at this point in their relationship.

Like why, having eased himself away from her body to go and shut out the sound of that screeching owl, had he not gone back to his own bed? She'd been sound asleep. It would have been the perfect moment to leave.

He glanced over to where Delphi was standing beside the small grey mare, his eyes following the soft, seamless movement of her hand.

But he hadn't. *He hadn't been able to.*

The idea of leaving her had made some kind of earthquake happen inside him, so that he'd had to sit down in the armchair to steady himself.

But why had he felt like that? Their relationship was over. They were getting a divorce. There was nothing left between them.

Liar, he thought, and before he could divert the direction of his thoughts he was back at the kiss he had been trying so hard not to think about. His heart thudded inside his chest. He could keep telling himself it had been just a kiss, but he knew it had been so much more than that.

Last night he had wanted her so badly his hunger had felt like a physical ambush. Truthfully, they had both wanted it—had both been waiting for it to happen since that moment on the field in Idaho when he'd pulled her into his arms. Having failed so spectacularly to do so in his marriage, he had wanted to prove a point—to pin Delphi down not just metaphorically, but literally.

With his mouth.

But, unlike in Idaho, last night there had been no point to prove. It had been simply an acceptance, an acknowledgment, an admission of a mutual need that was stronger than both of them. A surrender to that need to kiss and touch and caress and press against one another that was ever-present, circling them constantly, whipping at their senses and nudging them closer, like the rope Delphi had lightly flicked into the sand to make Alima move.

And she'd tasted so good. Hot and honey-sweet. And the taste of her had gone straight to his head.

In those few febrile heartbeats nothing had

mattered except the sweep of her tongue against his and the fierce hunger raging through his body. Five more seconds, maybe ten, and he would have stripped them both naked and slid deep inside her.

That he had not done so, but instead had taken her arms and held her away from him, still stunned him now.

But, looking down into her face, he'd known he had no choice. Emotions—big emotions that neither of them knew what to do with—had been roaring inside both of them. He'd known in that moment that Delphi was vulnerable and that he couldn't exploit that vulnerability.

Remembering how she had fought him, how she had kept trying to pull him closer and how, shockingly, her cheeks had been wet with tears, he felt his chest suddenly tight, as if his ribs were in a vice.

He understood her longing to disappear, to displace those big, unmanageable feelings with something else. Something all-consuming like sex. For hadn't he felt that way himself? But instead of sex, for him it had been work. Empire-building. His need to catch his father's magpie gaze chasing him around the globe.

Not that there was any need to tell Delphi that. She needed support from him—not some two-bit excuse for the behaviour that had left her feeling so diminished and abandoned.

He stared across the sand school. Delphi was wearing that dress, the one from Idaho, paired with jodhpur boots. With her tousled short hair, she looked nothing like the woman sheathed in gold who last night had shone brightest in a room full of beautiful people.

A pulse of guilt beat through his veins. She'd looked like a child playing dress-up. And in some ways she was still a child. A scared, confused little girl, orphaned before she understood the meaning of the word, and then left in a terrifying state of limbo while a judge decided her fate. And, yes, Dan had got custody of her in the end, but like with Alima the damage had been done, he thought, his gaze moving between Delphi and the small grey mare.

For a moment he battled to keep his breathing steady. And now there was more damage. A lost baby. A broken marriage. A husband who'd made promises he had failed to keep. He knew that sex would have briefly blotted out the pain, but what about afterwards?

That was the reason he had stopped them going further.

That and the fact that, whatever he told himself, told *her*, he wasn't ready for it to be their last time.

Ducking between the rails, he made his way towards her. 'So, what do you think?'

She turned, and the look on her face was almost too much to bear.

'I'm guessing her last owner was giving her mixed messages and punishing her when she got confused. When any horse gets confused, particularly one this young, it panics and tries to save itself. Hence the bolting and the bucking.'

She moved out of sight behind the horse, and he shifted position, moving just casually enough that it wouldn't seem as if he was following her. But he was.

'Do you think she can get past this? Can she learn to trust again?'

He watched the pulse hammering against the delicate skin of Delphi's throat.

'That's up to you.' Her voice was scratchy when she answered, and her fingers twitched against Alima's shoulder as if she couldn't control them. 'She won't hold on to the bad if you don't.'

The breeze was lifting the sand around her feet now. Reaching out, he rested his hand on the mare's shoulder, a hair's breadth from hers. 'And what about us? Could we do the same?' he asked softly. 'Follow her example?'

A bird swooped over their heads into the

eaves of the barn and Alima jerked her head. He swore silently as Delphi moved her hand to soothe the horse.

'I don't know,' she said at last.

Her voice was bruised-sounding, as it had been last night, and as Alima shifted to nuzzle the side of Delphi's face he wondered if the mare had heard it too.

'But I do.' He ran his hands over Alima's smooth neck. It was that or place them on Delphi's shoulders, and he sensed it might be better to wait a moment before taking that next step. 'Look, I know I took things for granted before.' He took a breath, his mind a swirl of guilt and grief. 'And what happened in London was terrible. But what we have is too special to just throw away.'

She bit into her lip. 'Divorce isn't about throwing things away, Omar. It's about acceptance and change.'

'And so is marriage,' he countered. 'Maybe it took all this for me to realise that, but now that I have, I can change. I am changing. I was trying to change. That's why I bought this place.'

She stared at him in silence, and he felt a flicker of panic. After last night he had thought that something had shifted between them, but now he could feel the past hanging over them like a mourning veil. He needed to make her understand that things would be different. That he could be different.

'I used to come up here with my older brothers to ride and climb and swim in the *wadis*.' It was here that he had felt closest to them, for they too had been dwarfed by the mountains. 'I'd been looking for somewhere to buy for some time, and then I saw this and it was perfect.'

There was a small silence; he made himself wait.

'Perfect for what?' she said finally.

'For us. For you. The Lulua is fine for overnight stays, but I wanted to give you a place where we could come, and it would be just the two of us and the mountains and the sky.'

More than just the two of them.

After years when the future had been a blank spot in his mind's eye, blotted out by the weight of expectation in the present, he had planned for a family.

'It was supposed to be a surprise. I was going to bring you here on our wedding anniversary. Only then you left.' His eyes found hers. 'I understand why. I didn't then, but I do now. I know I wasn't there for you. I should have been, but I wasn't. I let you down. I made assumptions.'

'Assumptions?'

The sound of her voice made his heart skip a beat. 'I guess I thought it would be easy to get you to trust me. I knew you'd been hurt in the past, but you trust Dan and your brothers. And I've watched you walk into a schooling ring with horses that were dangerous, and you trusted them not to hurt you.'

'Because they didn't,' she said quietly.

'I know. And I know I did. I messed up. But I thought, after last night… I thought there was a chance. I thought maybe we could… That we might try again. Try and fix things.'

Last year he had given a TED talk, speaking fluently for nearly twenty minutes on the importance of perseverance. In comparison, this was the least eloquent speech he had ever given. But for some reason he couldn't find the right words, so he held out his hand instead, just as he had watched Delphi do so many times when she worked with a head shy horse.

Heart beating unsteadily, he watched her face, silently willing her to take his hand, and finally, just when he had given up hope, she did.

His fingers tightened around hers.

'I've learnt from my mistakes. I made bad decisions, wrong choices, and I'm going to make better ones.'

'I made bad decisions too.' She bit into her lip. 'I was too scared to let you in, so I pushed you away instead.'

'And I deserved it. I'm not surprised you left me.' He hesitated, and then, reaching out, he stroked her cheek. 'I've missed you so much, and from now on things are going to be different. I'm going to change.'

Suddenly he tensed, his chin jerking up like Alima's had moments earlier—except it wasn't the shadow of a bird making his nerve-endings quiver but the sound of his phone. Glancing down, he felt his heart begin to race. It was Rashid.

'What are you doing?' asked Delphi.

He had pulled his hand free of hers and now it froze in mid-air. What *was* he doing? For the first time, probably ever, he and Delphi were talking. But, having seen the caller ID, he couldn't not answer any more than Delphi could ignore a barn full of horses. Besides, it would only take a few minutes.

'I need to take this. It's my father. I spoke to my father about settingup a meeting for me with Ali Al-Hadhri.' He saw Delphi was staring at him blankly. 'He's an intermediary for several key media conglomerates in the Middle East—'

'When?' She cut him off. 'When did you speak to your father?'

He frowned. 'This morning.'

The look on her face felt like a punch to the head.

'That's what you were thinking about this morning?' Her voice was thin and brittle. 'A business meeting?'

Clenching his jaw, he shook his head. 'That's not what I said. My father called me. He suggested the meeting.'

'And you didn't think to say that you had more pressing things to discuss? With me?'

She was staring at him as if what he was saying made no sense, and a part of him knew that it didn't. But the sound of his phone was tugging at his senses like a dog on a leash, so that it was impossible for him to think about anything but answering it.

'I don't have a choice, Delphi. You don't mess around with men like Ali Al-Hadhri. All I need is five minutes…'

He turned away from her angry, pinched face.

As predicted, the call took five minutes. Hanging up, he glanced at his watch. Four, in fact. Although judging by Delphi's narrow-eyed gaze that was four minutes too long. But it was done now.

He held up his hands in a gesture of apology. 'Okay, I admit that was bad timing, but that call was a one-off. It won't happen again—'

'Are you listening to yourself? How is this you changing?' Shaking her head, she gave a bitter laugh. 'You know, when you said you could change, I thought about last night and I believed you. I thought about this fort, and why you bought it and, idiot that I am, I let myself think that you meant what you said. That what we have is special. Only then you took that phone call. We were in the middle of a conversation about getting back together and you broke off to set up a business meeting.'

'It was four minutes, Delphi. And it was important.'

'More important than our marriage. That wasn't a question, by the way. I know that compared with business I am nothing to you. And I know that nothing I do or say will ever change that. Because you can't change. You won't stop until you have the biggest media empire in the world. And even that won't be enough. You'll probably have to go into space and see if you can set up a cable network on Mars. Omar Al Majid—media master of the universe.'

'You think that's why I work? For status and power?'

Of course she did. She couldn't know that he was driven by something more basic, more fundamental. The need of a child for his father.

So tell her, he told herself. *Tell her the truth.*

Except he had never admitted that to anyone. To the wider world, even to his closest family, it was something he held close. Only Jalila had ever sensed the root of his obsession with work.

Delphi's eyes were like fierce dark flames.

'Yes—yes, I do. I think you have to be on top of the podium, and that's what this is really about. Not me…not us.'

With an effort, he kept calm. 'I'm trying to save our marriage, Delphi.'

Her mouth trembled. 'No, what you're doing is telling someone who got bitten by a shark not to worry about going back into the water.'

He took a step closer. 'Aren't you the one who told me that sharks are the most misunderstood animals in the oceans…possibly the planet?'

She stared at him; he saw that her whole body was trembling now.

'Try telling that to someone who's been bitten by one. Look, I know this is hard for you to accept, but you can't win this one. There's nothing to save. You just proved that by answering that phone call.'

'You can't give up on nine...nearly ten months of marriage because of one four-minute phone call,' he protested.

'I'm not. I'm walking away from something that doesn't work. We don't work together, Omar. We don't want the same things. We can't be what each other needs. You just don't want to admit it. You don't want to admit that we failed because you don't know what it feels like to fail, to not be good enough.'

Something serrated scraped inside him at the flatness in her voice and he felt a flicker of panic. Or was it another emotion? He seemed to be spilling over with them right now.

'How can you say that after last night?'

'I'm saying it *because* of last night. Standing at the edge of an abyss is not the sign of a happy marriage, Omar.'

Her face was pale, and he could see the walls that had tumbled last night were back up—just as high and wide as before. 'Me coming here was never about saving our marriage. You wanted me to talk to you, and that's what happened, and now we're done.'

'That's not all that happened. You cried, and I held you, and if I hadn't stopped it, we would have made love.'

'And what if we had?' Her brown eyes were wide with frustration now. 'Do you think that would have changed anything? It's just chemistry, Omar. Or nostalgia. It's meaningless.'

She turned swiftly away and began leading the horse towards the gate. He swore under his breath and stalked after her. Using her arm and her momentum, he drew her in hard and fast against his body. He watched the anger in her eyes darken, saw her pulse accelerate in her neck.

'You think this is meaningless?' He felt the wind on his neck, but he didn't care. He only cared about proving her wrong. His hand slid over her collarbone and he felt her breath shiver. 'That you can get this anywhere? With any man?'

He felt a pang of jealousy—the same as he'd felt when he had seen her first wearing that dress.

'No, I don't.' She pulled away. 'But it's not enough.' Her voice sounded like the sand blowing across their feet. 'There has to be more.'

'We have more. We ride. We eat. We laugh. We talk.'

'We talked once.'

A gust of wind blew across the sand school. 'It's a start.'

Delphi shook her head. 'No, it's the end, Omar…'

Her voice petered out and she stared past

him, her forehead creasing into a triangle of confusion.

'What?' He frowned.

'Where have the mountains gone?'

Now he was confused. He turned—and felt his stomach turn to stone. She was right: the mountains had disappeared. In their place was a huge, rolling russet-coloured cloud, as wide as the horizon, filling the sky.

'It's a *haboob*. A dust storm.' He turned back to Delphi as another gust of wind swirled across the sand. 'Take Alima inside. Close the barn doors. Then go back through to the house and stay there.'

Gazing up at the quivering sky, Delphi felt her heart slow. She had thought a dust storm was just a strong wind. But this looked more like a tidal wave or some monstrous creature.

Behind her, Omar was shouting orders in Arabic at the men now moving swiftly across the yard, picking up stray buckets and bolting gates.

Talking soothingly to Alima, she led the horse back into the barn and into her stall. Against the gale, it took all her strength to pull the huge barn doors across, and incredibly the wind was getting stronger and louder by the second. Outside the air was growing hazy. The men were starting to lose their shape.

Her heart gave a lurch. *Where was Omar?*

Without thinking, she ran back outside.

It was like stepping into another world. Actually, it felt like the end of the world. The noise was deafening, and the air was churning with dust and debris. Choking, she staggered forward, lifting her arms to shield her mouth and eyes. Not that she could see anything.

She felt a flicker of panic. The barn had vanished. There was just swirling sand and the screaming wind tearing at her skin.

She turned, trying to get some sense of direction, but in zero visibility the five yards back to the barn might as well have been five hundred miles. She was dizzy, disorientated. And then a driving gust of wind made her stagger and she fell forward, coughing.

'What are you doing?'

A hand caught her elbow and hauled her upright. It was Omar.

'I told you to go back through to the house.'

Bent almost double against the wind, he was propelling her forward now, and she felt a sharp relief as the barn loomed into view.

'Get inside!' Omar shouted.

As she nodded, something dark and blurred

spun through the air and slammed into his side. He grunted in pain.

'You can't go back out in that!' She clutched at his arm, frantic with fear, as he turned towards the storm.

'I'll be fine. Go into the house.' His eyes were narrowed against the wind and he was having to shout above the noise.

She shook her head. 'No, I want to stay with the horses.'

She had never heard him swear, but he swore then—using a word that Dan had sent her thirteen-year-old self to her bedroom for saying.

'I can be with them.'

He pushed her back into the barn, but as he turned to step back outside, she clung onto his arm. 'I want to stay with you.'

The words came easily, just as if they'd been waiting to be spoken, but he didn't react, and she thought they had been lost on the wind. And then he was pulling the doors shut.

The noise dropped a notch and her hand tightened on his arm. 'Did everyone get inside?'

He nodded. 'They know the drill. Better still, they follow it.' A muscle beat in his jaw as he stared down at her, eyes accusing. 'What the hell were you thinking, going out there in that?'

'I didn't know where you were. I couldn't see you.'

His expression was unreadable. 'I thought you didn't want to see me.' Their eyes met and then he looked away. 'I'm going to check on the horses.'

Heart hammering, Delphi stared after him. Outside the wind had settled into a kind of rasping howl, and most of the horses were stamping and moving uneasily. Only Alima seemed unperturbed.

Omar shook his head. 'Brave as well as wise,' he murmured.

He reached out to stroke the mare's velvety muzzle and Delphi felt her spine turn to ice. On the front of his shirt, which should be yellow, a patch of red was spreading out like spilt wine.

'You're hurt.'

Looking down, he frowned. 'It's nothing. It's just a scratch.'

'You're bleeding. That's not nothing.'

There was a first aid kit on the wall next to an empty stall. A defibrillator hung beside it. As he tugged his shirt over his head, she felt a thud of shock. There was a graze along his abdomen—not deep, but ragged and oozing dark blood.

'It looks worse than it is.'

Trying not to fall into the gap in her mind where all the bad things were buried, she cleaned the wound and applied a sterile dressing. But as she pressed the edges against his smooth golden skin, she couldn't stop imagining what might have happened. What she knew could happen. And the possibility of that seemed enormous, rising up and crashing over her, sweeping everything away.

'What if it had hit your head?'

'It's okay.'

The concentrated gentleness in his voice made her hands start to shake. 'I couldn't see anything.' Her heart was pounding inside her chest. 'I couldn't see you.'

He pulled her into his arms. 'I know.'

Tears clogged her throat, and she pressed her hands against his chest, his shoulders, his beautiful undamaged face, needing to feel him, to check he was okay. 'No, you don't understand. I can always see you. Even in the dark…even with my eyes shut. Only I couldn't then.'

He stared down at her, his eyes burning black in the dim light.

'But I could see you.'

Everything stopped.

The wind outside paused, and the world hung motionless.

She held his gaze, and her breath, and then their mouths met blindly, greedily, urgently, and she melted into him.

CHAPTER EIGHT

OMAR LEANED FORWARD, backing her against the stable wall, one arm moving to brace himself against the wood, his tongue parting her lips to deepen the kiss. It was as if he had lit a fuse, and she felt a tingling heat sear through her straight to her belly.

She moaned as his lips moved across hers, teeth catching her lower lip, and then he tipped back her head and he was kissing her neck, his mouth pressing against the pulse beating wildly beneath her ear.

Shivering inside, she arched against him, her nipples hardening as they brushed against his smooth bare skin, and she shuddered at the sensation, nerves, need, anticipation swamping her.

His fingers had found the zip of her dress and he was working it down her back, pushing the fabric away from her shoulders. A shiver of anticipation rippled over her skin as it fluttered to the floor, but Omar did nothing. He just gazed down at her simple white underwear, breathing deeply, a dark flush fanning across his beautiful cheekbones.

Everything about him was beautiful, she thought, her head spinning as she looked up at him. He murmured some words in Arabic, a language she could neither speak nor understand. But she didn't need to do either to know what he was saying. His eyes made it clear, and she felt heat flood her limbs as his dark gaze slid down her body.

Her eyes never leaving his face, she slowly toed off her boots, then reached behind her back to undo her bra, letting it, too, slip to the floor. Heart thudding, she touched his chest. His skin was incredibly warm. She could feel his heart beating beneath her fingertips, and lower down it was as if his hand was already stroking her belly…smoothing her hips. Cupping the slick heat between her thighs.

She shivered, her breasts aching, body tense. Damp. *Yes*, she thought.

And then her breath caught as he reached for her, scooping her into his arms and carrying her into the empty stall. He kicked the door closed behind them and set her down firmly on a pile of hay.

Dragging in a breath, she pulled him to his knees—not gently. She wanted him…wanted to be completely his—physically, at least—and she clasped his face, kissing him fiercely, her hands reaching for the button of his jeans.

As her fingers slid beneath the waistband Omar groaned against her mouth, and then he was batting her hands away and holding her still, a storm of passion in his dark eyes.

'Are you sure this is what you want?'

His voice was hoarse, as if the sand had chafed his throat, and she could feel the effort it was taking him to hold back.

'I've never been surer of anything.'

She pressed her hand against the hard outline of his erection and that was all it took to accelerate him. He slid his hands beneath her panties, drawing them down her thighs and lowering his weight against her. His mouth found hers. His lips and tongue were urgent, his body hot and hard, his hands cupping her breasts, stroking, shaping them.

Heat was lapping over her body like waves curling onto the shore's edge and hollowing out the sand, and she sucked in a sharp breath as his mouth closed over one taut nipple, licking, nipping, teasing the swollen tip, before switching to the other.

Curling her arms around his neck, she pressed up against him, her body so sensitive now that she wanted to tear off her own skin.

He made a rough sound in his throat, and she felt his palm slide over her abdomen to brush the wet curls at the V between her thighs. Then he parted her legs and she jerked, body twitching, as his fingers flexed inside her, then stilled. Helplessly, she lifted her body, wanting more, wanting the ache pounding through her to be answered.

'Omar…'

She whimpered his name, the muscles inside her clenching with frustration, and then his callused thumb began moving in slow circles that made her tremble inside. Moaning softly, she moved her hand to his groin, and she felt him tense as she pulled him free of his trousers, her fingers curling unsteadily around him. She had forgotten what it felt like to hold that length of smooth, polished flesh in her hand. The power and the thickness of him.

He grunted and jerked backwards. 'Wait,' he commanded.

She watched him strip off his remaining clothes, and then he was lowering himself down onto her body, lifting the hair from her neck to kiss and suck her throat. Heart hammering, she raised her hips and stroked the blunt head of his erection against her clitoris, moving it back and forth.

Omar gripped her hand, his ragged breathing vibrating against her skin. 'I don't have protection.'

She felt a momentary flicker of indecision. But she wanted him, without barriers of any sort, and so, shaking with need, she pulled him closer, cupping him in her hand. She felt his body tense and his control snap, and he gripped her hips and pushed inside her.

A moan of pleasure escaped her lips. The waves inside her were getting bigger, sucking her back further. This was what she wanted. *He* was what she wanted. Her fingers bit into his shoulders as he began to move against her, thrusting deeper, then withdrawing to thrust again more deeply still. The waves were moving faster and faster, feeling hotter, so that she was panting now. And just when she thought she couldn't take any more those waves crashed over her, embracing her, and her back curved upwards, her body gripping his tightly.

As she shuddered against him, she felt his lips brush against hers and he groaned out her name and thrust upwards, surging inside her.

They lay together, panting shakily, their bodies hot and damp with sweat, muscles twitching.

Outside, the storm raged on. Not that she noticed. Lost in the white heat of their passion, there was only her and Omar. Truthfully, the *haboob* could have peeled off the barn roof like the lid of a sardine tin and neither of them would have noticed.

She felt Omar shift his weight and then he rolled sideways, taking her with him, still inside her. *Still hard.*

Her heart skipped a beat. Her body felt wonderful, as if all the tension of the last few days had been ironed out of her, but her head was spinning. What had she been thinking? Having sex without protection was not just stupid but reckless.

Only it didn't feel reckless. It felt right.

More than right.

After weeks and weeks of feeling broken and scared, she felt complete. Safe. *Happy.*

Just like she had in Vegas, when Omar had slid the ring on her finger. When they'd run hand in hand through the hotel corridors to their ludicrously over-the-top honeymoon suite, she had got so close to believing in happy endings, so close to believing in the two of them, in the possibility of their future together.

And now, lying here, wrapped in his arms, their bodies fused, it was so tempting to let herself believe the same.

But she hadn't known then what she knew now. That even if somehow, they could put the past behind them a future was no longer possible.

What had happened in London had changed everything. Or maybe it wasn't that it had changed everything so much as shown her what was real and possible and what was just fantasy.

Her heart began to beat faster. She knew everything there was to know about fantasies. Ianthe and Dylan had been a Romeo and Juliet for the social media age. Two photogenic lovers: unfiltered in life, undivided in death. Tens of thousands of words had been written about their tempestuous relationship, and their most devoted fans might still want to believe their affair had been a real-life fairy tale.

But as far as she was aware there were no stories about Sleeping Beauty sleeping off a hangover, or Prince Charming being too stoned to go to the ball.

The wind was drumming against the roof, but not loudly enough to drown out the pounding of her heart.

As for their tempestuous relationship: with hindsight it was clear that her parents' arguments had been inspired not by passion but by alcohol and insecurity. Their rows had been frequent and explosive, but the next day it had always been as if all of it—the shouting and the screaming and the door-slamming—had never happened.

No wonder she found it so difficult to talk. To express her feelings. To say what she wanted. What she needed.

'Where have you gone?'

Omar's voice broke into her thoughts and, twisting round in his arms, she tilted her head back and met his eyes.

'I'm right here,' she said quietly.

The tension had left his body and it suited him. Relaxed, he looked even more sexy than normal, with his limbs resting negligently against the hay and his eyes dark and drowsy. Skin prickling, she reached up to touch his face, needing, as always, to check that he was real.

As if reading her thoughts, he pulled her closer, and her breath caught as his fingers moved lightly over her hip to caress her bottom.

'And so am I.'

Her heart thudded. Unlike her, Omar always knew what to say and how to say it. It was how he had got under her skin all those months ago, so that the barriers she'd built against the world softened and melted. But nothing had changed, she told herself. Not really. Whatever her body was saying. Which was lucky, she thought a moment later, as he shifted position so that her breasts brushed against his chest, and she felt her hips lift towards him without her consent.

'Can I get you anything? I'm not sure I can offer much, but there's a fridge in the office.'

The lazy softness in his eyes reached out to her, and she felt fingers of heat tiptoe over her skin 'Some water would be great. I'm just so thirsty suddenly,' she lied.

'Okay.'

She had wanted him to move and put himself out of temptation's reach, but as he got to his feet, she felt the loss of his sleek, hard body like the amputation of a limb. Then, to add insult to injury, she had to watch him walk away, and her mouth felt as if it had been sandpapered—which served her right for lying.

Don't look, she told herself.

But it was impossible not to. Not to savour his gorgeousness. Except for his silver wedding ring he was naked, and with his rippling muscles and smooth golden skin he was as gloriously, unashamedly male as the stallions in the neighbouring stalls.

And he was still aroused.

She squirmed against the hay, her insides liquid and hot. *As was she.*

'Here.'

Omar was back. He handed her a glass of water, and she took it, trying not to look at his body as he sat down beside her. The water was ice-cold and she drank it thirstily, wishing it could satisfy all her needs.

'Is there anything else you want?' he asked, pulling her close.

Yes, she thought, imagining his hands on her belly, and on her hips, and between her thighs. But it would be greedy and stupid, as well as irresponsible, to let anything happen again. And yet the idea that this was their last time together made her feel so miserable that her skin could barely hold it in.

'What is it?'

Omar touched her wrist, and there was a tension in his hand that made her look up at his face. He was staring down at her, his eyes moving over her, through her, as if he was seeking something.

'I didn't hurt you, did I?' he said finally.

She frowned. 'Hurt me?'

His gaze held hers. 'I should have checked everything was okay. After the miscarriage, I mean. But I didn't think… I wasn't thinking.'

That made two of them, she thought. Why else had she not stopped when he'd told her he had no condoms? There was no good answer to that question, so she pushed it away.

'Everything's fine; you didn't hurt me.'

Above them, the sand sounded as if it was scouring the roof.

'Except I did, didn't I?' His voice sounded scoured too, and taut, as if it was an effort to get the words out. 'I hurt you, and I'm so sorry for that, Delphi. I am so very sorry.'

She stared at him; her pulse suddenly featherlight. Omar had apologised so many times in their marriage, but usually the 'I'm sorry' had been followed by some conditional clause that largely exonerated him from whatever had upset her. Because, of course, the real problem was her inability to trust and confide in him.

So now she waited for the 'if' or 'but' to follow his apology. But he didn't say anything like that. Instead, he bent his head. 'I'm sorry,' he said again. 'I should have been there for you, and I wasn't. I let you down.'

With the barn doors closed and the air outside dark with sand there was not much light in the stable, but there was enough for her to see the strain in his face. And the remorse.

Her heart beat in the darkness. She hated it that he was hurting, even though he'd hurt her. 'And I should have told you I was pregnant.'

He shook his head. 'I'm not just talking about the baby. Last night, when I was watching you sleep, I kept thinking about all those business trips I took. All those times I was late home or didn't come to bed. It never occurred to me how hard that was for you.'

Delphi swallowed. Her throat felt tight, and her stomach lurched a little as she remembered all those long evenings and weekends alone.

New York was only an hour away to the family ranch house in Bedford, but it had been harder than she'd thought to live in the city. Hard and terrifying to leave her father and her brothers and the home that had been her sanctuary for so many years.

'It was all right at the beginning…' When she'd thought his long working hours were necessary. When Omar had made them sound temporary. 'But then it wasn't.'

His dark eyes met hers.

'I know. And I know you probably don't believe me, but it was never meant to be like that. I just wanted to take care of you, and I told myself that was what I was doing…that I was being a good husband even though I was hardly ever there. I knew you were homesick and lonely, but I was too thoughtless to admit that I was the one making you feel that way.'

'I *was* homesick and lonely…' It had been more than that. Over time, it had felt as if she was losing her substance. 'And scared.'

'Of me?'

The shock in his voice wrenched at something inside her.

'No, not of you. Of having made the wrong decision.'

Again.

She thought back to Vegas, remembering the intensity in his voice as he spoke his vows, the feeling of her blood pounding round her body. She had been full of love, full of hope.

Afterwards, in the weeks when she should have been honeymooning with Omar, she had felt both lonely and fraudulent. As if she was exercising squatter's rights not just on the coolly beautiful Manhattan apartment, but on the idea that she could be happily married to a man she loved.

'I thought our marriage was your priority… that I was your priority. That's what it felt like before the wedding. Then everything changed on our honeymoon. I thought that once you made that deal it would go back to how it was. Only it didn't. It just got worse. You were always at work, or away on business, and even when you were there you were working. I suppose it just ground me down.'

She felt his spine go rigid, but for the first time in their relationship he didn't attempt to defend himself.

'And then, after London, I was just so tired.

I couldn't do it anymore. I couldn't keep telling myself that it would work when I knew that you wanted something more or different. So I left.'

The white-hot pain of leaving him had been offset by one tiny, frail hope.

'I thought you'd come after me,' she whispered.

She heard him take a breath.

'I thought you'd come back,' he said. 'So I waited. And then I was so angry with you for not staying and fighting for our marriage that I thought I'd make *you* wait.' His mouth twisted. 'Only you'd been fighting for months, and I didn't know because I wasn't there. I was never there when you needed me.'

Her throat clenched as she remembered something. 'You were there last night. I thought you left, but you stayed, didn't you?'

He nodded. 'There was an owl screeching, so I got up to close the window. When I came back you'd rolled over, so I slept in the chair.'

She stared at him, her heart leaping against her ribs. 'I thought I was dreaming.'

The intensity in his eyes scraped under her skin. 'I couldn't leave you. I couldn't walk away. And I never stopped looking for you either.'

His hands were clenched, and his face had lost colour. Heart thumping, she gazed up at him, thinking back to the complicated series of choices and omissions that had brought them to this point.

Could she walk away?

But she knew the question that needed asking was not *could* she, but *should* she? And the answer to that hadn't changed. Because deep down she knew that he couldn't be who he wanted her to be, and he wasn't what she needed.

That admission knocked the air from her lungs, and suddenly she was desperate to stop thinking and feeling. Eyes stinging, she pressed her finger against his mouth, quietening him.

'We both made mistakes.'

But she wasn't going to make yet another one by thinking that this quivering, mind-melting, incessant pull between them was something more than it was. More than it had already failed to be. More than it was capable of being.

They had reached the end, and there was no point reading anything into the fact that they were here, together, naked in this stall. What was happening in this little bubble was not real life. It was understandable, excusable. *Human.* A reaction to the hostility of what was happening outside. Two people trapped in a storm, hunkering down together, bodies surrendering to their lingering sexual longing for one another…

So make it about what it was, she told herself. *Make it about sex. And passion. And heat. And need.*

Pulse leaping, she placed her hand against the hard muscles of his stomach and glanced up at the roof. 'How long will the storm last?'

He followed her gaze. 'It's difficult to say. I could go and take a look outside in a bit.'

'There's no rush.' Her fingers walked down the vertical line of fine dark hair arrowing across his stomach. 'We have shelter and water.'

Something flickered in his dark eyes. 'And you think that's enough?'

There was a second's silence and then his hand moved to her hip, and she felt a rush of hunger flare inside her.

'It could be a long night.'

Her gaze roamed over his beautiful naked body. 'I think we can probably think of a way to pass the time,' she said softly.

Leaning forward, she wrapped her fingers around the smooth length of his erection. She heard him swallow, and then his head dipped, and he was clasping her face and kissing her. She told herself that was what she wanted. She wanted to be kissed. In kissing, she could forget everything—the good, the bad, the ugly and the beautiful.

He pulled her closer and she felt him press against her belly, hard where she was soft and yielding.

Tomorrow she would leave. But first there was this. One last night together in the eye of the storm. She arched into him, her body melting, seeking blindly for the oblivion of his mouth, her heart beating with hunger and relief as, angling his head, he took what she was offering.

Turning his body away from the shower head, Omar closed his eyes and jabbed his fingers through his hair to remove the last traces of shampoo.

It was the morning after the night before.

The storm had lasted until dawn, the raging wind alternating with short pockets of calm. Thankfully, the first rays of sun had woken them early, so that by the time his panicky staff had opened the barn doors he and Delphi had been fully dressed.

Unlike last night.

He felt his body harden.

Their coupling had been like a storm within a storm…their desire as hot and fierce and relentless as the wind. Jolted to the core by a hunger that had circled them for days, they'd touched and teased and tormented one another, changing position, losing themselves in the rhythm of their pounding hearts and hips, pausing to catch their breath or a few minutes' sleep until need drove them on again, only stopping when their aching muscles and chafed skin had forced them to.

His groin twitched and he pressed his hand against the blunt end of his erection as if to stifle it. Delphi had been like quicksilver in his hands, white-hot, her body quivering and arching against his, her soft moans of pleasure sweeping over his skin like tiny dancing flames licking at the logs in a grate.

He hadn't been able to get enough of her. He hadn't been able to taste her deeply enough. His desire had scraped him raw. Her desire had cut him loose and left him spinning, adrift in the dark of the barn.

And now, incredibly, he was aching for her again.

Gritting his teeth, he flicked the shower control to cold and, without flinching, let the freezing water course over his naked body.

Last night had unleashed more than that boiling, twitching hunger. Or perhaps it was more that unleashing it had swept away all the confusing detritus of their marriage, crumbling it into sand. And in that clean, uncluttered landscape it was easy to see that his previous assessment of his role in their marriage had been biased, not to say inaccurate.

He had always considered himself to be a civilised man, a good husband, a perceptive and attentive partner. But this morning, as they'd made their way back to the fort, he had been forced to rethink that assumption, and the truth was that he had behaved badly. Selfishly. Unkindly.

Instead of supporting her, he had hurt and confused her so badly that she had shut down, and he hated it that she'd felt that way—hated knowing that *he* had made her feel that way. For so long he had blamed her past for the obstacles that lay between them. But he had been equally to blame, if not more.

Delphi was right. Work was his obsession—an obsession she could see, anyway. And over time he had let it consume him, and bumped Delphi to the bottom of his agenda.

Remembering how he had taken that call from his father out in the sand school, he felt his face burn with shame. After weeks of separation, and months of being at odds with one another, they had finally been talking openly, honestly, about their marriage. Delphi had been holding his hand. The last thing he should have done was answer his phone, but he had reacted unthinkingly, ruthlessly turning his back on her, driven by a need that outweighed everything in his life—even his wife.

It hadn't started out that way.

Meeting her at the Amersham, he had been smitten, mesmerised, and the fact that she had neither encouraged nor welcomed his attention had only cemented his desire to change her mind. He had dropped everything to pursue her.

She had become his new obsession.

Even now, picturing their wedding, he could feel the relief, the almost orgasmic ecstasy of a marathon runner crossing the finishing line first. But three days later, prompted by a phone call from his father, he'd cut short their honeymoon and flown off to secure yet another in a long line of empire-building deals.

And Delphi had returned home.

Alone.

All the time he'd been promising to be by her side, pressurising her to trust him, telling himself that he was taking care of her, protecting her from the world. But he had been the one hurting her. Jaw clenched, he dipped his head beneath the spray of water. He had spurred her on. But at the same time he'd leaned back and pulled on the reins.

He had confused her, and she had tried to save herself.

Like Alima, she had bucked, and then bolted.

And she would have bolted again yesterday, except the storm had made leaving impossible.

He switched off the shower and leaned forward, watching the water swirl down the plughole.

And now?

There was an ache in his chest that made it hard to catch his breath. The idea of her moving on and making a life without him was agonising. He wanted her to stay more than he had ever wanted anything, but if he wanted that to happen then the conversation he had started out in the sand school would have to be finished.

Only this time he would let nothing get in the way.

Wrapping a towel around his waist, he took a breath and walked back into the bedroom. Delphi was standing on the balcony, and his pulse soared as she turned towards him. She had showered first and was still wearing his bathrobe, the sleeves rolled up, the hem grazing the floor. With her slightly damp hair and bare feet she looked incredibly sexy.

Her gaze rose to meet his, and a faint rose-coloured flush crept across her cheeks. 'I was just looking outside. It's like the storm never happened.'

He glanced past her at the cloudless blue sky. It was a perfect summer's day. There was no reason Delphi couldn't leave. What mattered, though, was giving her a reason to stay. The thought made his heart thump.

'It's hard to believe, isn't it, that something that intense doesn't leave a trace?'

He saw her gaze move to where the towel clung snugly to his hips, and she frowned.

'But it did.'

He followed her gaze, glancing down at where the skin across his abdomen had turned plum-coloured. 'It's just a bruise.'

Without apparently moving, she had drifted closer, and for a few agonising half-seconds he thought she was going to touch the bruise. But then her hands fisted at her sides.

'Last night, you said it was just a scratch.'

'Which only goes to prove what you already knew,' he said.

'What's that?'

Her brown eyes were glittering, but her mouth was soft and vulnerable, and everything inside him slid sideways—just as it had that first time at the Amersham, when she had made an entire polo match, complete with ponies, players, and spectators, disappear.

'That I don't always know what I'm talking about. That I get things wrong. And I *was* wrong, Delphi. About so much. I know that I confused you, and I hurt you, and for a long time—too long, in fact—I didn't even see what I was doing. But I do now, and nothing is more important to me than you.'

Beside his bed, his phone buzzed once.

Watching Delphi's face tense, he took a step closer, as if doing so might reinforce what he was about to say.

'And if you'll give me a second chance, I promise things will be different—*I* will be different. Let me prove to you that you can trust me.'

Now his phone started ringing. They both stared at it and he almost laughed—although nothing about the situation was funny. He wanted to break the tension between them, and the only other way he knew to do that was by kissing her. But if their marriage was going to work it, sex couldn't be the only way they communicated. He had learned that much in the last few days.

Snatching up the phone, he switched it off and tossed it onto the bed.

'You didn't have to do that,' Delphi said stiffly.

'Yes, I did, and I should have done it a long

time ago. But now I need to do more than just tell you that I can change. I need to show you. I need to show you that our marriage matters more to me than anything else. That you matter more than anyone else.'

All the time he was speaking she was still there, and that was all that mattered. Keeping her here. But he'd realised that he was telling the truth. For the first time in his whole life, nothing—not even his father's approval—was as important to him as Delphi and their marriage. He wasn't interested in who was calling him or what they wanted.

She was shaking her head, her eyes too bright. 'Don't do that. It's not fair.'

'I don't care about fairness. I care about you.'

'You hurt me.'

His heart contracted. 'I know.'

'And then I hurt you. I don't want us to keep hurting each other.'

'I don't want that either. But if you leave now, do you think the pain will go away?'

'No. But sometimes hope is more painful than loss.'

Her raw admission made his pulse quicken and, cupping her cheeks, he tipped her face up to his, refusing to let her look away. 'But our hope survived the storm.' He stared down at her. 'You're the beat of my heart…the air I breathe. And I know I've been selfish, and I'm still being selfish in asking you to stay. But I don't have a choice. Because I—'

Because I love you.

He stared down at her, his heart pounding, the unfinished sentence booming inside his head, shocked. But why? He had never stopped loving her—even when he'd been furious and hating her for leaving him. But Delphi was so ready to run, and big words like love had always scared her. He couldn't risk scaring her now.

'I need you. Without you, nothing matters. I don't matter.'

Panic had made him careless, and his throat tightened. It was his worst fear—one that he had never admitted to anyone—and the idea that he had just done so to Delphi made his stomach churn.

'Of course you matter,' she said hoarsely.

'Then stay. At least for a few weeks.' His thumbs caressed her face. 'I still owe you a honeymoon, remember?'

'A honeymoon?'

Hearing the longing in her voice, he felt his body tighten. She was so close that he could feel the heat of her, see the pulse beating in her smooth throat, the conflict in her eyes.

'I can take you anywhere. We can go back to Maui.'

She bit her lip. 'I don't want to do that. I want it to be about us. Not fireworks or acrobats. Just the two of us, spending time together. Both of us present, not hiding or distracted.'

Omar nodded slowly. She was right, and it sounded so easy—only he knew he was treading on eggshell-thin ground. They could go anywhere in the world. All it would take was a phone call. But why go anywhere? Why not stay, and spend time together here?

'Then could I show you around the city? I don't mean the malls or the fountains or the Burj. I mean my Dubai. The place where I grew up.'

Her eyes were tired, but he saw a flicker of curiosity, and he took a deep, burning breath as he realised just how scared he'd been up until that moment that she would leave him.

'I'd like that,' she said quietly.

'Then that's what will happen.'

His voice shook a little and he leaned closer, needing to touch her, to check that she was real and that she was still his.

As if sensing his thoughts, she looked up into his face. 'This is just a trial, Omar. I can't… I don't want to make any more promises.'

'I understand. All I want is a second chance.'

Their eyes met. 'Is that all you want?' she asked slowly.

Omar stared down at her, captivated by her question and by the rise and fall of her breasts beneath the robe. He waited a moment, and then he reached out and undid the belt around her waist. Breath bottled in his chest; he slid his hand beneath the soft linen. Her skin was hot and smooth like satin. He touched her breasts, feeling the tips harden beneath his fingers.

She moaned and tipped back her head, exposing more of her throat, and then the robe slid from her shoulders, and she was naked.

Their eyes met, and then she reached out and unhooked the towel from his waist. It joined the robe on the floor. Now they were both naked.

He sucked in a breath, and then he was nudging her backwards, and her hands were pulling him down onto the bed, shaking with eagerness, and then there was only Delphi, and the cool sheets sliding beneath them, and the pure, pulsing beat of their desire.

CHAPTER NINE

TURNING HER HEAD, Delphi breathed in deeply. The air was so different here from the mountains. There it was clear and dizzyingly fresh. But this was different with every breath. There was salt and spice and the fumes from the various boats chugging up and down and across the choppy waters of the Dubai Creek, or the Khor Dubai, as it was known locally.

It was two days since she and Omar had emerged from the barn into the daylight. But they had survived more than one storm. And the second—the one that had taken place in the bedroom—had been infinitely more terrifying and painful.

Honestly, she hadn't believed him when he'd said he wanted to change, that he *could* change. But when it came to it, it didn't matter. She didn't know if it had been the desperation in his voice, or the smudges under his eyes, but she hadn't been able to walk away.

Her heart bumped against her ribs. She still didn't know if she had done the right thing by staying, but she did know that walking away wasn't the solution anymore. It never had been, only she hadn't been able to see that then. She had been too locked into her own fears, too scared to take a risk. But something had changed—she had changed. And he had too.

And now she was sitting in an *abra*, one of the flat-decked wooden boats that ferried people from one side of the creek to the other, with Omar's hand wrapped around hers, breathing in not just the air but the sights and sounds of the waterfront.

There were hundreds of wooden boats tied three deep along the creek, and on the quayside, men were ferrying boxes of shirts and milk powder and cooking oil on their shoulders.

And, as if all that activity wasn't incredible enough, they were alone.

Or at least it felt as if they were alone. The bodyguards were still close by, but Omar had insisted that they blend in. She glanced over to where he was sitting beside her, his gaze tracking the movements of the river traffic. They were supposed to be doing the same, but it would take more than a baseball cap to make Omar Al Majid blend into any crowd.

'What do you think?'

She felt him shift closer and she turned, her heart making a startling leap into her throat as their eyes met.

'I think it's amazing,' she said truthfully. 'It's so busy.'

Omar had been right. This was nothing like the Dubai she had seen on the way to the Lulua. There were no glittering skyscrapers or glossy supercars. Everything was brightly coloured and there was so much to see.

'It's like this day and night. The people who live and work here never stop.'

'So where are we going first?' she asked as he helped her disembark on the Deira side of the creek.'

'The market. Although it's not quite like the farmer's market in Bedford Hills.'

Her chest felt tight, as though it might burst. It had been one of her favourite places to go with him before they'd got married. But those lazy mornings spent browsing handmade cheese and local honey had been swept aside and forgotten, like everything else.

Or maybe not forgotten, she thought now, as his hand tightened around hers and he led her through the crowded, labyrinthine lanes.

First stop was the cloth market. Every single space was occupied. In some places bolts of vividly coloured textiles were balanced in unsteady piles against the walls, in others they spilled onto the streets. There was barely standing room and the noise was astonishing.

'Is that Arabic?' she asked, as a woman began to shout at a man who was holding up a pair of beautiful, embroidered slippers.

Omar shook his head. 'Urdu. But around ninety per cent of the population is expat, so you'll hear a lot of languages. You get used to it.'

'Is that why you're so good at languages?'

He seemed surprised by the question. 'Not at all. I'm only good because I had so many extra lessons. It's not something that came naturally to me.'

'But you wanted to get better?' It was typical of Omar that even as a child he had seen it as a challenge to overcome. 'And you worked hard to get what you wanted?'

Next to her, Omar was silent, and she sensed a tension that hadn't been there before.

Then he said, 'It was my father who wanted me to get better, so that's what I did on my weekends. I learned German and Mandarin and Spanish and French.'

It didn't sound like much fun. It didn't sound like her weekends on the ranch… 'Wouldn't you have rather been playing with your friends?'

'Of course. All I wanted to do was play football and polo. But it's been very good for business.' He gave her a small, tight smile. 'Shall we move on?'

Very good for business, she thought, but surely that couldn't have been Rashid's intention.

After the cloth market they made their way to the souks. Omar had been right, Delphi thought, gazing at the crowded stalls. It was nothing like the farmer's markets back in the States.

'This was part of the old Silk Road,' Omar said, leading her through the throngs of shoppers. 'Goods from all over the world have been coming through here for centuries. For a few decades Dubai was Deira.'

As they wandered down one alley after another, Delphi found herself falling under his spell again. She loved the sound of his voice, the strength of it. Most of all, she loved the fact that there was no agenda, no pressure to move on—and she was finding out things about him. Stupid, small things that glowed in her mind like the jewelled necklaces in the gold market.

'What is it?' she asked.

They had stopped to drink coconut water at a stall, and Omar had been gazing down at the green coconut in his hand. Now he looked up at her, smiling, and the sudden softness in his face pierced her heart.

'I used to come here with Hamdan when I was very young,' he told her. 'He'd pick me up after school and get the driver to drop us off. I remember being so excited by how they chopped off the end of the coconut with a huge knife.' He shook his head. 'I'd forgotten all about that.'

She smiled. 'Why did Hamdan pick you up from school?'

Omar stared past her into the bustling market. 'He didn't always. But my dad worked away a lot, and when he travels, he likes to have his wives with him. Hamdan was married by the time I was six, so I'd go and stay with him and his wife.'

Delphi stared at him, replaying not only his words, but what Jalila had said at the party. 'You said "when he travels", but he doesn't still travel for work, does he?'

His face stiffened a little. 'Sometimes. He gets a lot out of it.' He pulled her against him. 'Now, can I tempt you with something a little spicier?' he said softly.

As his dark eyes rested on her face she felt her heart start to hammer inside her chest. She was almost desperate to feel his mouth against hers. 'I thought you'd never ask…'

The spice market was huge and open air, but the alleys leading to and from it were so thick with scent she could practically taste it on her tongue. There were bulging sacks of dried black limes, barberries, rose petals and rosemary.

Delphi rubbed some of the familiar needle-like leaves between her fingers. 'I thought this was more of a Mediterranean flavour.'

'They do use it in cooking, but it's also medicinal. My mother uses it for dizziness. Olive leaves… They're supposed to be good for the heart.'

She met his gaze, her own heart hammering. 'And what about all those?' she asked quickly, gesturing to the photo-op-worthy miniature cone-shaped mountains of heaped spices.

'That's sumac, ginger, cinnamon, *ras-el-hanout* and saffron. You have to be careful with saffron,' he added. 'A lot of it is fake. They use dyed cotton or shredded paper. That's why you should drop it in water before you buy. To see if it loses colour. The darkest is the best,' Omar said, pointing past her to a teetering burnt orange mound. 'And the real thing should have a splayed end. Oh, and you have to haggle,' he added. 'It's expected.'

But when he finally paid, she could tell the

vendor was delighted. 'I thought you said you had to haggle,' she said.

They were eating lunch at one of the waterfront restaurants, where *leqaimats*—seductively sweet dumplings drizzled with a sticky syrup—had followed a thin pancake filled with buttery tarragon-flavoured scrambled egg topped with shards of black truffle. Now they were sipping coffee.

He shrugged. 'I don't need to win at everything.'

Something stirred in her head. A memory of Jalila taking hold of her hands at Rashid's party and telling her how happy she was to see her brother in love. *'I know he's rich and gorgeous, but I also know how intense he can be, how fixated he is on proving himself.'*

How fixated he is *on proving himself*: present tense.

At the party, she had been too stressed to mull over Jalila's words, and afterwards there had been so much going on. Now, though, she had time to think. But the more she thought, the less they made sense. What did Omar have to prove now? He was wealthy enough to stop working tomorrow and still live a life of unparalleled luxury. And she had seen first-hand the reverence with which other important and successful people treated him.

'I still want to win. But I know that I have to stop, or it will ruin our future.' His hand tightened around hers. 'It almost destroyed our marriage. It's just hard for me to stop.'

There was a long, weighted silence.

'Why is it hard?' she said quietly.

But in her head she was wondering why she didn't already know the answer to that question. And why she had never thought to ask it before now. But then she had always been too busy resenting Omar, too distracted by her own feelings and thoughts to consider his. She had viewed their life together through the lens of her past, her pain.

But what about his past...his pain?

'It's been so long.' His beautiful mouth twisted. 'I was so young when it started. I don't even think it was conscious. I just slipped into it. It didn't matter when it was just me and my goal. But then I met you, and you made everything disappear. I couldn't stop thinking about you. I knew you'd been hurt but I thought that if I could get you to trust me, then I could take away your pain.'

'You did take away my pain.' She reached out and touched his hand.

He flinched. 'But I caused you pain too.' His voice was hoarse. 'I took you for granted. I told myself that marrying you was enough. That it proved how much I loved you.'

His words made her eyes sting, and she felt a rush of misery. 'It would have proved it to any normal person. But I was so scared of being let down that I couldn't let it mean anything.'

'Of course you were scared. What happened to you as a child was appalling. Of course it was going to affect how you see the world.'

'The world, yes. But you were my husband. I should have talked to you. I should have told you how I was feeling and asked about *your* feelings. Only I didn't try to fix things. It was easier for me to run and hide and blame you.'

'Because I am to blame.' His face was taut. 'I made promises I didn't keep. I said one thing and did another. I didn't plan for it to happen. But then, on our honeymoon, my father called.'

Delphi blinked, but she wasn't remembering that day on the beach in Maui, but her first meeting with Omar's parents in New York. Rashid had been distracted, hardly present, but Omar had been the polar opposite. There had been a tension in him…

'I remember,' she said quietly.

Omar nodded. A muscle was working in his jaw. 'And do you remember me telling you that it was an important deal? I told you it was necessary. I told myself it was a one-off.' He sucked in a breath. 'I was wrong.'

'You made a mistake.' She squeezed his hand. 'Your father must think very highly of you to bother you like that.' She wanted to comfort him, but instead she saw his shoulders brace against an imaginary blow.

'Not really. Mostly he struggles to notice me at all. Although, to be fair, it's not just me. But I suppose I struggle with it the most.'

Glancing up at Omar's face, she felt her heart tumble in her chest. His dark head was bent, and the strain in his voice was visible around his eyes, but she was seeing his face at Rashid's party, and the tension beneath the beautiful smile. The same tension that had held his body taut like a switchblade during his parents' visit to their New York apartment.

'Because you're the youngest?'

It was a hunch, but he nodded.

'Everything I did had been done sixteen times already. Nothing I did mattered. And it was worse when we were all together. My brothers and sisters were always so much bigger and louder and more articulate than me. When I was with them, I felt like I was lost in this crowd. It was like nobody could see me or hear me.'

Tears filled Delphi's eyes. When she was a

child that had been her dream. She had longed to be invisible. But never from Dan or her brothers—just the wider world: the gossip-hungry public and the paparazzi who fed that hunger.

She glanced over to where their coffees sat cooling on the table. 'Do they know how you feel?'

He shrugged. 'Jalila does. And Hamdan. They understand. But it wasn't the same for them. Jalila is one of seven, and Hamdan is one of nine. When my dad went away on business, or stayed at the other houses, it didn't matter so much to them. But there was only me and my mother, and when he wasn't there my mum found it hard. That's why she would go away with him on business. Only then it was like I was living in this huge, empty mausoleum. That's why I used to go and stay with Hamdan.'

Her chest squeezed tight. At the margins of her mind, things were falling into place. Like how he hated coming back to an empty apartment.

'It sounds awful.'

She felt his grip on her hand tighten.

'To be honest, it was worse sometimes when he was there. I was so desperate to get his attention, but then there was the pressure to keep him interested. And I never knew when he was going to leave, so I used to follow him around, because I was paranoid he would go without saying goodbye. Which he usually did.'

Delphi felt her stomach clench. And she had done it too—and hurt him by doing it. Only she hadn't known she was hurting him in that way. Hadn't known she was pressing against an old bruise. She had been too wrapped up in her own past even to consider that he had bruises too.

Her face must have shown some of the shock she was feeling, because he gave her a small, tight smile.

'I don't want you to think he's a bad father, or that he doesn't love me. He's not and he does. And it's not all his fault. He's ninety years old, and he's been preposterously rich since he was younger than me. That means he's always the most important person in any room. Maybe not always—I mean, he does know heads of state and kings. But most of the time people treat him like a king, and so he acts like one. He never has to wait for anybody or anything, and if he gets bored then he just moves on to the next thing.'

He stared past her at brightly coloured *dhows*.

'The trick is having the one thing in the room he's curious about…'

And now, finally, she understood the long

hours and the late nights. 'That's why you work so hard. To build something that holds your father's attention.'

He nodded. 'He ran a newspaper at university, and he loved it, but other things happened. He got into property and shipping. But he always had a soft spot for news and media, and I suppose I picked up on that. I did a stint at the *Crimson* when I was at Harvard, and I liked it. So when I got offered a chance to buy up a bunch of local news stations across the US, I took it.'

The intensity in his eyes transfigured his face.

'It was probably the first time I'd ever held my father's attention to the end of a conversation.'

She could hear the wonder in his voice. The wonder of a little boy finally managing to balance the obscure, complicated equation of novelty and challenge that held his father's gaze.

'That must have felt amazing,' she said quietly.

She couldn't imagine Dan acting that way. He had always put her first and centre stage. Her brothers too. But there had also been space for her to become her own person.

'It did. I've never done drugs, but I guess it was like a high. And I was hooked. Like you said, I became obsessed. It was all I thought about.'

She stared at him. 'I don't remember you being like that when we met. I don't remember talking about work at all.'

'That's because when I met you it was like being born again. Nothing before you mattered. I was completely smitten. I actually thought I was going mad because you were always in my head. I could always hear your voice, see your face.'

His eyes rested on her face, dark, steady, blinking.

'Normally when I met a woman even before she opened her mouth, I knew who she was. But with you I felt like I was trying to catch a kite by the tail. You were this beautiful wild girl, riding bareback, and every moment I spent with you was a breath of mountain air.'

Delphi stared at him without blinking. Her heart felt as if it was on fire. For so many weeks she had pushed away those memories. Now, though, they broke through like a river bursting its banks.

'I felt the same way. It was as if my whole life up till then had been lived in a gale. I was always fighting just to keep on my feet. And then you came along. It was like the wind dropped and I didn't need to struggle any more, because you were there, and everything was so calm and quiet and safe.'

Omar lifted her hand to his mouth and kissed it softly. 'I'm so sorry I hurt you. It makes me ashamed, thinking about how I behaved when you've gone through so much. So much loss. So much pain. I've lost nothing. I had no right to feel like I did. To do what I did to you.'

'You were lost. That's not nothing.'

Around them, the noise of the creek was fading. The stevedores and the fishermen were just blurred figures, moving as if through water. The cacophony of language and dialects was a faint hum. It was just the two of them now.

His dark eyes rested on her face. 'But then I found you, and I wanted to be everything to you. I wanted to be your everything. Only I knew you were holding things back. Dan told me to be patient. That you weren't the kind of woman I could put reins on. But I didn't listen. I just kept pushing and pushing you… Only then I pushed you too far and you left.'

She breathed out shakily. 'After London, I just gave up. But I was wrong to leave. I should have stayed and told you how I was feeling. I should have told you that I needed you. That I loved you.'

His dark eyes reached into her, holding her

still. 'And what about now? What are your feelings now?'

Tears were running down her face. 'They haven't changed. I still love you.'

More even than she had before, because now she knew the real man she was loving.

'And I love you.'

For a moment, neither of them could speak. Then Omar cleared his throat. 'I want to kiss you so badly, only I'm not sure I could stop at kissing you, and I don't want to end up breaking any public decency laws.'

The huskiness in his voice as much as his words made her pulse leap. 'Maybe we should head back home.'

The corner of his mouth lifted, and his gaze, so full of love, reached inside her. As much a part of her as her love was a part of him.

'There's no maybe about it.'

* * * * *

If you were wrapped up in
Their Dubai Marriage Makeover
then make sure to discover the magic in
these other Louise Fuller stories!

Italian's Scandalous Marriage Plan
Beauty in the Billionaire's Bed
The Christmas She Married the Playboy
The Italian's Runaway Cinderella
Maid for the Greek's Ring

Available now!